**W9-BUV-602**

CANCELLED

# The Texan Rides Alone

# OTHER FIVE STAR WESTERN TITLES BY LAURAN PAINE:

*Tears of the Heart* (1995); *Lockwood* (1996); *The White Bird* (1997); *The Grand Ones of San Ildefonso* (1997); *Cache Cañon* (1998); *The Killer Gun* (1998); *The Mustangers* (1999); *The Running Iron* (2000); *The Dark Trail* (2001); *Guns in the Desert* (2002); *Gathering Storm* (2003); *Night of the Comancheros* (2003); *Rain Valley* (2004); *Guns in Oregon* (2004); *Holding the Ace Card* (2005); *Feud on the Mesa* (2005); *Gunman* (2006); *The Plains of Laramie* (2006); *Halfmoon Ranch* (2007); *Man from Durango* (2007); *The Quiet Gun* (2008); *Patterson* (2008); *Hurd's Crossing* (2008); *Rangers of El Paso* (2009); *Sheriff of Hangtown* (2009); *Gunman's Moon* (2009); *Promise of Revenge* (2010); *Kansas Kid* (2010); *Guns of Thunder* (2010); *Iron Marshal* (2011); *Prairie Town* (2011); *The Last Gun* (2011); *Man Behind the Gun* (2012); *Lightning Strike* (2012); *The Drifter* (2012)

# THE TEXAN RIDES ALONE

## A WESTERN STORY

## LAURAN PAINE

**FIVE STAR**

*A part of Gale, Cengage Learning*

GALE
CENGAGE Learning·

Detroit • New York • San Francisco • New Haven, Conn • Waterville, Maine • London

GALE
CENGAGE Learning®

LIBRARY OF CONGRESS CATALOGING-IN-PUBLICATION DATA

Paine, Lauran.
    The Texan rides alone : a western story / by Lauran Paine. —
First edition.
        pages ; cm.
    ISBN-13: 978-1-4328-2635-2 (hardcover)
    ISBN-10: 1-4328-2635-2 (hardcover)
    I. Title.
PS3566.A34T455 2013
813'.54—dc23                                              2013005467

First Edition. First Printing:June 2013.
Published in conjunction with Golden West Literary Agency.
Find us on Facebook– https://www.facebook.com/FiveStarCengage
Visit our website– http://www.gale.cengage.com/fivestar/
Contact Five Star™ Publishing at FiveStar@cengage.com

Printed in Mexico
1 2 3 4 5 6 7 17 16 15 14 13

# THE TEXAN RIDES ALONE

# Chapter One

Furred with the dust of travel he topped the gentle roll of land at its peak and saw the long shallow breadth of land that was like a valley between two breasts; one he sat upon, the other lay across the valley a strong mile. In between was stark greenery, vivid and clear under the thickening weight of a threatening sky.

He sat his tired horse, a limber Texan with blue eyes hooded behind the half-drooped eyelids. Behind him lay bitterness, inside him was acid triumph that he could fade into shadowy places, a swamp, a spit of trees, or he could outride the devil or outshoot men who had teethed on guns. He had come through pursuit with a whole skin but he was as tucked up in the flank as the horse he rode.

Rancor rode with him because he had run and it wasn't his way. In him, deep down, was boldness. Closer to the surface there was cruelty. Externally there was a dauntless scorn and an iron mirth in his eyes, a strong, willful thrust to his lips, and a ruthless jut to his jaw. If tenderness was there, it didn't show. Not over a hundred and eighty pounds of him was punched down inside a tawny hide that bulged with corded toughness, all of it several inches under six feet.

The gun on his hip rode at a daring slant, the ivory butt yellowed, well forward. His saddle was a Texas center-fire, oxbow stirrups, A-fork with the rigging up and around the horn. It had a Texas roll to the cantle and Texas brush marks, deep scores, scratched into the skirts, the *rosaderos*, from breaking through a hundred brush patches—sage, manzanita, scrub oak, bitter-brush.

The horse was slightly ewe-necked, long-legged, and lean like a Texas prairie wolf made for stamina, speed, not looks. He carried a split-ear headstall, a beautifully silver-inlaid Spade bit, and a dainty bosal across his nose. Everything but the man was Spanish-Texas and there was no mistaking the man: a brush-popper, Texican, restless within the law, a scourge beyond it.

Behind him the sky lay leaden, as gray as the travel stain upon the man and horse, its swollen, distended belly low. In the coarse air was the scent of rain. No wind, no sound, no stirring, just a rank grayness that made the valley below stand out the greener and upon the high roll of land, the Texan. He and the storm were arriving in Marais Valley.

He drew in a great gulp of the stillness and exhaled it. The horse's head was low, pointing down to Marais Valley, scenting the sweet grass. The Texan crossed both hands on the saddle horn and watched the softly unfurling view come up to him. The land lay north and south, great upthrusts of hills lay east and west. The valley itself was a hidden place, isolated with an air of serenity to it he could feel, absorb.

The threatening day with its winteriness enhanced the great splash of dark emerald down below. Distant trees that grew solemnly along twisting roadways, by clear-water creeks, stood out darker, motionless, before the dark-scudding clouds. He imagined the lonely moon coming up over all this, blazing with silver intentness in a vast stillness.

A hushed breeze ran ankle-high through the dead grass upon the ridge, made a sound as it leaped over the near edge and threaded its way downward toward the valley. He heard it, felt its residue across his face, smelled the roiled dustiness of it heavy with the metallic scent of rain.

Behind him lay a flat, sere country where scrawny-muscled

men lived with their fierceness. Down in the valley the men would be like their stock, well-fed, content, unstirred. He knew just from looking—the enduring patience, the everlasting sameness of security that permeated everything in Marais Valley. Even the Comanches rarely raided here, you could tell. Vaguely he saw two sets of buildings at opposite ends of the valley. At their sight the valorous shadows in his blue eyes shone, grew darker in hard amusement. Some men sought peace like this— some didn't. He lifted his reins and the horse moved out, sought a deer slide, and went skittering down it, legs stiff, bunched up, a miniature avalanche rattling behind. Another horseman would have sought a safer way down the hill.

He turned easterly across the valley floor, went slowly through the warmer, sheltered land until he met a road that lay torpidly crooked like an old brown snake, the rare glint of stone in its coarse, mottled, snakeskin markings. He rode down the lane that seemed to wander in tree-speckled shade forever until he saw a horse just off the road in among the trees, saddled but riderless. His left foot was swinging free of the stirrup, his body going sideways, hand running for the gun he wore, when the rider came around from the offside of the horse and stared at him. A girl.

He caught himself, moved his hand away from the gun, and felt for the stirrup with his toe, gazing across the narrow road at her. The urges of a bold and solitary man would always close down and block out other things when he saw such a woman. She was young and had hair as dark as midnight, with dew on it. That's the way it shone where in the fullness of the day the pattern of tree shade she was standing in was reflected off it.

There was a rich roundness to her. Girlishness, but with more fullness, more womanliness, that reached out to him across the dun-brown roadway and stirred him, making the flash of his eyes warmer. Her mouth was closed, the lips willful, full, and heavy with a beauty that hung in his throat and her eyes, black-gray to match the day, were level and appraising.

The way she caught his glance, held it the way a man might do, challenging something she saw in his face, accentuated the tension in the electrically charged atmosphere around them, in the hushed, motionless, withheld breath of the creeping storm. Her hand was square and strong, the fingers with a capable bluntness to them. She was a picture framed among the trees in the wild sullenness of the day, before his hungry eyes. When he broke the spell, spoke, sound splintered the gloom that lay in layers around them.

"Trouble, ma'am?"

And the bold blue eyes showed no shame at his thoughts. The scorn in them dared her to interpret what was there.

She answered without dropping her eyes, without moving an inch. "My horse is lame."

Easing his weight forward a little he said: "How far have you come?" Then he saw that the shoes were new. A bruise then. Maybe a pulled tendon, bucked shin.

"Not more than a mile." She still kept her level look of challenge.

He swung down and crossed over near her. She wasn't more than two inches shorter than he was. A tall, handsome woman. He looked away from her, down at the horse's favored leg, held out his reins, and said: "Here." She took the reins, moved aside a little.

He tugged up the right front leg and used a twig to dig around the frog, clean the hoof down to the sole and out to the edge of the shoe. There was no fever. He dug closer, flicking out grit. Wedged deep in one quarter lay a triangular, flinty little stone. He worried it free and held it in his hand. Every step had driven it deeper into the soft parts. He dropped the hoof and turned to her. She was close to him. Her eyes dropped to the stone on his palm and for a moment something strange was balanced in her mind. She didn't speak.

He looked at the dark profusion of lashes down over her eyes, at the lips lying closed, but without pressure, full and heavy. Her head came up as though a warning had sounded and he saw the widening of her eyes, the veiled abruptness of want in their depths. He closed his fist around the stone, put both hands on her, swayed her in until he could feel the sturdy beat of her heart through his shirt. He kissed her fully and fiercely on the lips, and stepped back.

She stood like a pillar and, looking squarely into his face, said: "It was easy, wasn't it?"

There was bitterness without anger in her tone, high color in her cheeks.

He could feel the shame come out of her and burst up against him. It made his own coiled cruelty flame up and he wanted to hurt her so he smiled; the squareness of his teeth, white in the russet of his face, flashed. He moved closer to her again, arms hanging loosely at his sides. He saw her nostrils quiver, but she took no backward step. Her fragrance swept over him.

"It was easy, all right."

She moved then, brought up a flashing hand that seemed to hover just in front of his face. He caught it, forced it down, down, until her knees bent and pain flooded her eyes. Then he let go. The smile was still in his face.

"You don't want to do that," he said. "You want to do *this!*"

He kissed her again, still holding the stone in his fist, and her mouth trembled, parted, under the savage pressure. Her breath broke, became ragged on his face. When he stepped away, he held up his fist before the tumult of her blouse, opened his fingers, and let the stone fall. It was rough and sharp and her eyes mirrored the shock, the tiny pain of its passage. He walked back to his horse, toed in, and sprang up.

From the saddle he gazed down at her without smiling, with a scorning lift at the outer edges of his mouth. "You're something a man could dream of a hundred nights in a row," he said in his too-gentle Texas way, "but right now my horse is hungry and so'm I."

He lifted the beast into a smooth lope and went down the little road, around a long bend and out of sight. Just the sound of hoofs lingered and that didn't last long because a soughing wind, full of sadness, slow and heavy, went through the trees around her and washed away the sound of the Texan.

Down the road a mile, he came to a great sprawling ranch where decay showed in gentle unkemptness. The barn was gray-white, bleached out, sucked dry of sap and colored like old bones. It stood huge and sightless—timeless—its walls of log and its pitched roof of curling shakes waiting with indestructible calm for the wrath of the storm to come. The house, across the barren yard with its small litter of cast-asides, was built on the ground, low, with a gallery that ran completely around it. There, the look, the feeling of decay, was the strongest. Two old hunting dogs eyed the approach of the Texan without rising or sounding. A flourishing rosebush with a trunk thicker than a man's wrist clung to the middle upright of the front gallery, its scent almost overpowering in the torpid stillness.

Four riders were leading horses to a gigantic sycamore tree where their saddles lay tangled in the dust. Each of them studied the Texan from beneath hat brims and nodded back when he nodded, like all cowmen have always done, welcoming and appraising at the same time, saying nothing so that their minds could weigh and sort out and total up what their eyes saw.

He drew up near them. "Boss around?"

A tall, older man, lean as a barley straw with upcurling hair over his ears and a good-natured mouth below steady eyes, answered. "If you want the foreman, I'm him. If you want the owner, he's at the house."

"Obliged," the Texan said, and rode to the house, stepped down, and left his horse standing, hip-shot and patient. He was almost to the porch when a hulking man, stooped, grown fat, appeared in the doorway, gazing at him. The big man pushed past the door and said: "Howdy."

"Howdy. I'd like a bait for me and my horse."

The big man nodded absently, lifted a bloodshot gaze, flung it over where the riders were mounting up, then dropped it to the Texan's face again. "Sure," he said indifferently. "Help yourself at the barn, then go around back to the kitchen. No charge."

The Texan took his horse into the shadowy old barn where an aroma of hay lingered, stalled him, fed him, hung his gear on a peg, and stood in the gloom, looking out into the gathering darkness, tasting iron in the air. It would rain like a fat cow wetting on a flat rock, directly.

The riders were jogging northwestward. His eyes sharpened briefly, watching them. They would have to ride for three days before they'd find anything, and then they wouldn't if they weren't looking. Texas was big.

He was in no hurry to go around to the kitchen. A big fat raindrop the size of a Mexican spur rowel splashed upon the ground just beyond the barn's maw. He heard the bursting sound it made and looked down. Dust rode atop the bubble like yeast until the earth sucked the water down, absorbed it, leaving just a dark, uneven circle. He looked up. The sky was moving sluggishly, like an undertowed ocean, uneasy, round to bursting, the color of pig lead, the kind from which he'd molded bullets.

A groping wind, slow and bumbling, stirred the sycamore's leaves high overhead and dragged its belly across the roof of the barn, making a dismal, haunted echo inside the structure. He listened and looked around him. Silence hung over everything, lending substance, reality, to the signs of decay, improvidence, indifference around the ranch. It was almost as though he were alone in the world, as though there wasn't another person on earth. The feeling dwelt in him, deeply born from the solitude, the isolation, the black-brooding storminess.

A hard sliver of thoughtfulness widened behind his eyes. He was three days from pursuit. It would die away; the riders would go back to Colville. Life would go on. Colville would forget a man with a smoking gun, and if he rode a thousand miles farther, he wouldn't find a better place than Marais Valley in which to lose himself.

He went around to the kitchen, met the cook whose watery eyes took in the appearance of him bodily, but lingered longest on the ivory-butted gun worn forward, and the Texan doubted that the cook pegged him as any grubline rider, some stray horseman in search of a bait for his horse and himself.

The cook angled his head sideways to indicate the long table. He didn't speak. The Texan crossed the room with the sound of his spurs, loud and musical, dropped his hat, and sat down. The cook sliced great slabs from a cold roast and flicked them onto a plate with the tip of his curved knife. He slid the plate in front of the Texan and drew off a mug of coffee from the ever-simmering two-gallon pot on a back burner of the cook stove.

The kitchen was man-kept. It was clean, but not severely so. The kitchen was another sign that this was a man-run ranch—stomped-out cigarette scars on the floor, a cook that chewed tobacco in the kitchen, the cast-asides in the yard.

When the cook resumed his own cup of coffee, he faced the Texan and his rheumy eyes were strictly appraising, neither friendly nor unfriendly. "Looking for work?" he asked.

The Texan looked up. The cook was a big man. He was old, weathered, faded-looking. His mouth was hidden by a beard and the Texan guessed it was down-drooping at the corners.

"Maybe. This place need a hand?"

The cook mocked him softly. "Maybe."

"What's it called?"

"The Proctor place. Brand's MVP. Marais Valley Proctor."

"Proctor's the owner?"

"Yeah. Walter Proctor."

The Texan resumed eating, remembering the big, puffy man who had met him at the door. After a while he said: "Does Proctor do the hiring, or is it the foreman who wants a hand?"

"They both hire. The foreman's Slim Thatcher."

"And you expect they need a man, eh?"

The cook's sardonic watchfulness deepened. "Big outfits can always use a *good* man," he said with leaden emphasis.

The Texan stood up, put his hat on the back of his head, and took the plate and cup to the washtub. "Well," he said, fishing for his tobacco sack and looking straight at the cook. "I reckon they need me, then."

He went outside, stood on the back gallery, and lit his cigarette. The big raindrops were falling all around him now. The smoke from his cigarette went straight up, hit the gallery ceiling, and mushroomed outward. The air was still. Southward from the house ran a sea of grass, dark green, pastern high, rippling under the raindrops. A thick voice spoke behind him.

"Understand you're looking for work?"

It was the big man, Proctor.

"Do you need a man?"

"Yes, we need a man," Walter Proctor said in his slow, thick way, troubled gaze steady, as still as the air they were standing in. "We pay forty dollars a month, found, and feed for two horses."

"I've only got one horse," the Texan said, boldness in his eyes. "Make it forty-five, found, and *one* horse."

Proctor's eyes flickered but he didn't hesitate. "Forty-five for one month," he said. "If you prove up, it's forty-five from then on."

The Texan smiled with scorn in his face. Colville had made him $7,000 in forty minutes. He dragged long on his cigarette, hearing the rain like drumming hoofs on the roof. And Colville was why he was in this hidden valley, too.

"All right, Mister Proctor."

The big man turned toward the back door. "When the boys come in, see the foreman, Slim Thatcher."

The Texan watched the door shiver behind Proctor and smiled without humor, twisted back to watch the rain, finished the cigarette, and flipped it out where the downpour ground relentlessly against its hissing, sputtering protest.

Pulling his hat well forward, he went around the side of the house and across the yard to the barn. Rain darkened his shoulders, knocked little puffs of dust out of his hat, and flattened the shirt across the breadth of his chest. From beneath the hat brim he could see where the road curved, where the trees marched along on either side of it. Somewhere up there through the gray dismalness of the downpour was the northward reach of the valley. His instinctive knowledge of what all this would look like when summer finally came wasn't marred by the rain. It was a quirk of his, a flaw, being able to imagine things at their best, too strongly.

A little turn of the head from the doorway of the barn and he knew inwardly that MVP needed him, needed new blood. Maybe the whole of Marais Valley needed new blood. Or just blood. Sameness hung in the air, shone from the pools in the yard. Sameness, security.

He saw the lone rider coming through the rain, head down, hunched over, the horse tuck-tailed, shaking its head to keep rain out of its ears. His gaze closed down over the figure, blocked it into memory, and the rider never once looked up as the horse swung closer. The Texan stepped back into the gloom and let the animal go past.

He was still standing there when the rider unwound, hit the ground with a squishy, damp sound, and threw the left stirrup over the seating leather to tug the latigo loose. Then he saw the water-flattened blouse, the heavy contours beneath of a woman.

A cruel smile crept up to his mouth, stayed there until the girl had hung her saddle on its peg by the right stirrup, looped the bridle over the horn, and flung a soggy saddle blanket over it all, hazing her horse into a stall. As she turned, she saw him faintly, back there in the shadows, and her wet, shiny face, pale, grew still, her eyes up and level and darker gray-looking, like the barrel of a rifle at dawn.

They were twenty feet apart. The darkness silhouetted her, accented her tallness, her sturdiness, and what he imagined in his mind the rain-soaked clothing confirmed.

She stood like stone, heavy mouth like he remembered it, closed but without pressure, motionless, almost lifeless. He savored this moment of their second meeting. In a way, this was the symbol of his life; it was he who surprised her, had her unsure, wondering. It was always like that. The Texan's presence, his look, his gun caught others unprepared.

He didn't know that he looked handsome there in the gloom, teeth barely showing white and strong in the glow of sun-darkened face, ice-chip eyes unmoving, confident, that the rain-darkened curl of his hat brim framed his face with sinister grace, that his expression hinted things beyond the immutable laws of society to the girl.

He laughed and the sound was like a ripple of chains being drawn through the cannonade of the rain. It stung her to life. She moved, crossed the space that was between them, and went past him without looking around, out into the deluge. He saw her shoulders tighten under the lash of big drops. She didn't hurry. He watched her until she was a vague sapling being scourged far across the yard, then she was lost to him and faintly he heard a door slam.

# CHAPTER TWO

The Texan had another cigarette. He leaned in the doorway, smelling the fresh breeze that was cold and damp, when the riders came, slipping, sloshing their way through the storm like wind-blown phantoms emerging from an ocean. The horses grunted and shook themselves when they were in the barn, and the tall, thin foreman came over beside the Texan, wagging his head in a dripping smile. He was going to speak when the first deafening roll of thunder broke, boomed, trembled, made the barn quiver, and a second later a crackling dagger of blinding white light stunned them all into immobility. One of the riders farther back in the creaking barn cried out in a high voice and the foreman looked up into the guts of the sky where enormous ribbons of round gray writhed. In awe he said: "God damn, what a storm."

The Texan looked up only briefly. The second peal of thunder shook the world and he smiled elfishly to himself. The Comanches would be beating their foreheads against the ground today, scared silly. He laughed. The foreman looked around and into his face, his expression without humor. He said nothing. Of such first impressions are the skeins of acquaintanceship woven.

The men came trooping out of the bowels of the barn and clustered around their foreman. All of them accepted the presence of the Texan; they were too preoccupied with the magnitude of the storm to do otherwise.

When the lightning came splashing its wall of livid flame like

19

the eye-searing stroke of a master painter across the heavens, a man dropped his cigarette and flinched. He stooped, retrieved it, and looked straight ahead. Through the driving rain came a glowing orange light, square and strangely soft, from over at the main house.

The foreman shook his head again, twisted a less congenial glance on the Texan. "You staying over?"

"Mister Proctor hired me," the Texan said softly, still watching the ragged sky twisted in anguish.

"Oh." The foreman's eyes lost something from their depths, took on a more intent expression. After a moment he said: "Fetch your gatherings and come on over to the bunkhouse." He left, leading the other three men in a shambling, slithering run toward the building that stood, square and utilitarian, between the main house and the barn.

The Texan watched. The foreman's gaunt frame held his attention the longest. There was sardonic amusement in his face. He made no attempt to move until the riders disappeared with chilled yowls inside the bunkhouse, then he went deeper into the barn, down where the girl had put her horse, and there he leaned on the door, gazing at the animal.

A thin sequence of thoughts ran through his head keeping pace with the drumming rain. He finally turned away, went to his saddle, untied the saddlebags, and slung them over his shoulder. At the doorway he halted and bent a long look toward the house. So she was a Proctor. What kind of men did they have in Marais Valley that a girl like that one went wanting? Through the darkness the little lamp glow was warmly inviting. She'd be in there, dry now, perhaps with that great wealth of dew-black, shiny hair caught up and held, and the grace of her hidden in a long-flowing dress, the fire that only he knew about burning, high and hot, beyond the impassiveness of her face.

At least he pictured her that way. Pictured her with the stain of shame high in her face and the gun-metal gray eyes moving with dark-tortured memories of their kiss. And he knew that he'd come riding from Colville and blood and pursuit, down into the secret valley of Marais, to lie against a rich mouth and laugh at it. To share the secret of a beautiful girl. It had been so easy. Like he'd said too easy.

And her father, that big man with the puffy face and hop-toad gut, owned all this. This run-down barely ticking heart of an inland empire. He put the saddlebags down and made another cigarette with the fresh, cold breeze against his face. Lit the cigarette and let the smoke trail off and become lost in the washed night.

He conjured up a picture within his mind of the view he'd had from atop the barren hill. No, not all this, because there'd been another sprawl of old buildings away up the valley, northward. Half of it, then. Half of Marais Valley. His mind tightened down upon the picture behind his eyes. A man wouldn't share that girl's secret with anyone; he shouldn't share this valley, either.

He stooped, hefted the saddlebags, flicked back a strap, and peered in, ran his fingers down, down under the wad of things until they felt the crispness and in the murkiness he caught the glint of a paler green than valley grass. Colville's $7,000 lay under his hand. A hard thrill cut down across his nerves, ran out to the ends, and made him quiver. A memory of guns, of wind slapping him over the face, men lunging through the night after him, days of flight, of ruse, of doubling over old tracks, of finally losing them with an old trick—shedding his horse's shoes and driving some loose horses ahead of him. And now this— MVP rider, $45 a month, found, care for the ewe-necked horse.

He closed the flap, buckled it down, slung the bag across his shoulder, and shot a final glance toward the lamplight, stepped out into the rain, and felt its stinging, ruthless coldness on his face, against his clothes like a hundred tiny fists, and walked slowly toward the bunkhouse.

Inside a poker game was in progress. The guttering lamp hanging overhead sent up puffs of ragged black smoke from an untrimmed wick and in a corner of the room an iron stove was popping. Warmth fanned out through the place. There was man smell, and less noticeably horse smell. Slim Thatcher looked at the Texan with that hint of reserve and pointed his chin toward an empty bunk.

"That's the only vacant one. By the way, I didn't catch your name."

The Texan put his saddlebags on the bunk and spoke without looking around. "Merrill," he said, then sat on the edge of the bunk, removed his spurs and kicked them under the bunk.

The foreman was straddling a bench with the others. "I'm Slim Thatcher." He nodded toward a dark-visaged man with a puckered knife scar across one cheek. "Sam Oberlin." His eyes flicked to the youngest man in the room, who wore a perpetual and foolish grin. "Holk Peters. And this"—with a grimace toward the pale-eyed, badly warped man with the wizened face—"is Holystone. He got that name because he's got a medicine bundle he totes around in his pocket like a Comanche."

The man called Holystone looked down at the table until all the cards were dealt, then very slowly, slyly, turned his head and gave the Texan a raffish look, a wicked wink.

The Texan laid back on his bunk, watching the game. The air in the room thickened with tobacco smoke as time crept by and the undiminishing thunder of rain on the roof neither grew nor slackened. It held to a monotonous dirge. Intermittent thunder and lightning made shattering interruptions.

Holystone was cleaned out first. He turned around on the bench with a dead cigarette hanging from thin lips, showed good-natured acceptance of his losses, and studied the Texan's face for a long time before he spoke.

"New to the country?"

The Texan nodded lazily. "Yeah. I've been north and around about but never down here before. Wouldn't hardly have believed there was a valley like this east of the big river."

Holystone grunted around his cigarette, got his legs untangled, and thrust them out. He was in his stocking feet. He dug around in his pockets for a match, found one that only sputtered when he lit it, and threw it with a curse on the floor. He accepted the light the Texan offered, puffed life into the stub, and inhaled with satisfaction.

"It's quite a valley. Seen much of it?"

"No," the Texan said. "I came over that ridge to the west and there it was."

Holystone nodded vigorously. "Exactly the way I first seen it," he said. "Damned wind was a-blowing and I was stuck to my saddle with cold. Rode up a slope and there she was. That was wintertime, though, and man, the wind blows around here then." The faded eyes crinkled. "All you come through was a cussed thunderstorm."

Sam Oberlin looked up briefly from his cards. His dark eyes held a mocking geniality in their depths. "He brung it with him," he said. "Him and that damned storm come together, remember. We was riding out when they both blew in."

Holystone considered this for a moment, then grinned his sly grin at the Texan. "You did for a fact," he said. "Come with the storm. Stormy, now how's that for a handle?" He beamed at his own ingenuity, repeated it to the card players, and Slim Thatcher spoke without looking up.

"Fit better if his last name was Night."

"Makes no difference," Holystone said stubbornly. "Not a damned bit, no, sir. Stormy Merrill."

The Texan's face was partially hidden in the shadows of the bunk overhead. A little grin hovered around his mouth not quite settling there as he watched the work-warped older man across from him. The custom of the range was to nickname men for something they did or didn't do, for some idiosyncrasy they had. However ridiculous such a name—like Holystone— when it was bestowed, it meant acceptance. Right now that was one of the things the Texan wanted. Acceptance first, then security. The name, Stormy, offered one; MVP offered the other. The little grin settled and stayed.

"How many head's MVP run, Holystone?"

"Ask Slim. He'll lie to you, though, 'cause he don't know any more'n I do . . . or Walter Proctor, for that matter. Maybe three thousand head of cows and a hundred or so bulls. It's big enough," Holystone added with a twinkle, "to keep ten riders humping. Instead of ten, though, Slim and the Old Man'd rather work the bejeesus out of five men. Saves considerable money, y'see."

"Oh," Slim Thatcher said acidly, "you old windbag . . . shut up."

"See?" Holystone shrilled. "See what a rider's got to put up with on MVP?"

Merrill's smile grew, his bold blue eyes swept over the card players, and came back to Holystone. "Is there another ranch in the valley?" he asked.

"Yeah. Big B. Belongs to Colonel Buttrick. Home place's up the valley about four miles. Colonel and the Old Man sort of split the valley up between them."

"Is there a town in the valley?"

Holystone looked owlish. "Town? You sure are a stranger in these parts. Closest town's Fort Burnett, thirty-four miles north of here." The pale eyes with their secretiveness grew sly again, chiding. "But we ain't altogether cut off, Stormy. Rangers ride through every now and then, if that'll give you comfort."

Sam Oberlin's face was wreathed in tobacco smoke. His dark eyes lifted slowly to the Texan's face and stayed there. Hard, dour eyes. "This is a good country to be in," Oberlin said, then let his gaze drop back to the cards in his hand.

A twinge touched Merrill. He kept his gaze on Oberlin's face for a long time, probing both face and remark for meaning, but Oberlin didn't meet his look, appeared wrapped up in his cards. When his attention was drawn back to Holystone, there was something brittle and knife-edged in his mind toward Oberlin.

"When this rain lets up, you'll get an eye full of Marais Valley, Stormy," Holystone was saying. "Slim's about ready to work us to a frazzle on the spring marking bee." The bantering tone atrophied. Holystone grew pensive. "This has been a good winter, though. Never did get really cold. No snow to speak of. Open winter. There'll be lots of calves to mark, yes, sirree."

Slim Thatcher let out a rattling string of curses and tossed in his hand. "I'm licked," he said, taking up Holk Peters's tobacco, bending over it, fingers flicking like hairless spiders. "Holystone, why don't you go over and build a fire under Cookie. I'm hungrier'n a coming-out bear."

Holystone made a derisive sound. "You're so hungry, you go over. I'm not that hungry. Besides, I just dried out from that silly ride in the rain."

Thatcher looked at Holystone in disgust. "You're nothing but a grub bag anyway," he said, then a thought crossed his mind. The Texan could see its shadow pass over his face. When next Thatcher spoke, his voice had softened, become pleasantly warm and wheedling. "Holystone, you could give us all a sup of that whiskey in your war bag."

Holystone's raffish features pinched down hard. His eyes assumed their sharp, sly look. "That's for my lumbago and you know it," he said.

25

"Lumbago, my foot. What you got's a craving . . . not lumbago, you old sinner."

Sam Oberlin arose abruptly in dark fury. He was a poor loser at best, but when a downy-cheeked lad like Holk Peters beat him at poker, it bit down deep into his pride. His dark eyes glowed with a savage light, the scarred face twisted into the ugliness of scarcely held wrath.

Peters began a gloating and unheeding count of his winnings, and the Texan looked past him to Oberlin. Big, thick as an oak, Sam Oberlin looked to be a half-breed or a part-blood Mexican. There was tight-lipped, growling silence to his stance and expression. A primitive cleverness moved in his cold stare. There was a feline grace, a swiftness to his movements, and the Texan decided he had to have an Indian strain. No Mexican had the sheathed ferocity of Sam Oberlin.

Peters's drone went on unmindful of the swelling vein in Oberlin's throat. Holystone and Slim Thatcher saw it. Both cuffed Peters at the same time with their voices, told him to count silently. The boy looked up then, saw the black eyes boring into him, and stood up quickly, pocketing the money with a dull flush running under his smooth cheeks.

Then the cook hit the triangle a savage blow and the bunkhouse erupted men. Rain and fresh air gave everyone an appetite. Stormy Merrill was the last man through the door. Overhead the sky was breaking up into jagged, dire gray cloud floes, tossed and broken by a high, silent wind. The rain was lessening. The storm was all but past. He paused a moment, watching the scudding clouds. There was a smile on his face.

# CHAPTER THREE

Spring came on the heels of the last storm and the days flowed like water. Marais Valley warmed. Six MVP riders, including Cookie and Stormy Merrill, went out with a sprung-axled wagon piled with their gear, their irons and bedrolls and extra lariats, to mark and brand. They would be out three weeks.

It was around the faint coals after sundown that Stormy came to know Slim and Sam, Holk Peters, Holystone, and the cook, whose name, if anyone knew it, was buried under the designation of his trade—Cookie. The work was hard, the hours long, and out of the bruising punishment, the ribaldry, emerged a heel-and-horn duo of ropers whose infallibility pushed all other hopefuls into the background. Sam Oberlin would head, Stormy would heel. They would reverse, trying each other, waiting for a fumbled throw. Neither ever missed and out of this pairing up grew a silent and mutual respect, an aloof regard for one another as ropers. Top hands, both.

It was the eighteenth day out that the bond between them was sealed. Slim and Holystone were at the holding ground, circling the herd, keeping it milling, confined. Either Sam or Stormy would walk their horses into the herd, ease through slowly, gently, cut out a big calf to be worked, edge it toward the fringe of the herd, then jump it out into the open in a burst of speed. Like popping the seed out of a grape.

The other roper would be there, watching, waiting. A rope would hiss, a calf bawl in fright, and the other member of the

27

roping team would swoop in low, his loop hanging lazily then dropping, and a calf would be held by the head and heels, dragged up to the fire where Holk stood waiting.

Holk would move quickly to the struggling animal, shove a front leg through the noose around the neck to prevent strangulation, turn and bend over with his knife ready. If it was a bull calf, it emerged a steer; if a heifer, Holk ear-marked it, laid aside the knife, took up an iron, and burned MVP into its living hide, smoke boiling up around his sweaty face, into his stinging, reddened eyes. An undercut in one ear, a double-bit in the other. Branded, marked, altered if necessary, a wrench of the ropes, and the calf was up.

Then Sam brought out a short yearling, squirted him out of the herd, and Stormy was there. The rope went out, down, the dallies snaked over one another, and the calf let out a frantic bawl. Within the herd came the answer of a mammy cow. Sam Oberlin came in fast. His rope spun down hard, the calf's hind legs were in it, and Sam set his dallies. The big calf rent the air with a choking roar; Sam set back to spill him. His rope broke. Stormy had the full fury of the animal to occupy him. With a burst of fury Sam threw himself from the saddle, ran in cursing, big arms extended, fingers hooked. The calf jerked and plunged and just before Sam grabbed at him Slim Thatcher's scream shivered a wild warning over the dust and tumult.

A range cow with a calf was much more dangerous to a man afoot than a range bull.

Stormy heard the cry and saw the cow coming, slobbers trailing past her shoulders, legs pumping like pistons, horns a foot off the ground to disembowel Sam. His sweat-sticky fingers spun off the dallies. With a high-flaunting toss he threw the rope clear and spun his horse. Sam was half twisted, black eyes wide, seeing the cow's rush toward him. He perceived the red eyes, the slobbers, the murderous horns held low to rip upward.

Out of the churned dust Stormy loomed up. His horse's chest hit hard against the brute. She staggered, tried to swing wicked horns to gut the horse, but had been struck too hard, staggered, and went to her knees.

Stormy cat-footed his horse to block her head-on and roared at Sam: "Get on your horse!"

Sam ran. The cow got up slowly, shaken, bellowed for her calf, and turned with it beside her, trailing a length of Sam's rope, back toward Slim and Holystone, who were spurring up. She dodged them both and disappeared into the sea of shaggy backs.

Sam's jaw muscles were rigid, his eyes riveted to his saddle horn when the three riders converged upon him. Slim blew out a big breath, but said nothing. His face was pale. Holystone was swearing with fervor and incoherence. Stormy took out his tobacco sack and they could all see how rock-steady his hands were. He curled up a smoke and lit it, held the sack danglingly toward Sam, who also made a smoke with steady fingers, took a light, and over the flare of the match the black eyes held the blue ones in a long stare, neither blinking, then Sam nodded, inhaled, and straightened up.

"Well?" Slim saw the coiled spring of antagonism in the dark eyes, raised and lowered his shoulders, and jerked his head in silence at Holystone. They rode back toward the scattering herd.

"God damned cheap rope," Sam said savagely.

Stormy smiled thinly at nothing. "Bring back two," he said. "I'll wait for you at the herd." He rode away, and Sam's fierce gaze followed him a moment before the half-breed rode after two new lariats.

That night they seemed to favor one another a little at blackjack, and later, when the stars were out in a murky, glazed sky, they sat humped over, talking. Little snatches of conversation shot back and forth almost begrudgingly.

They were still sitting like that when Holk Peters and Holystone came in from the bedding ground and threw their saddles down, put their horses in the rope corral, and shuffled up near Cookie's wagon where Slim Thatcher and the cook were squat shapes under dirty blankets, sleeping. Holk went straight to his bedroll, but Holystone made a smoke and dropped down heavily near Sam and Stormy. He ran a leathery fist over his face and sighed.

"Your turn, fellers. They're bedding good, though. Nothing'll spook them tonight." He looked at the dark profile of Sam Oberlin. "If that wasn't the damnedest thing," he said mildly. Sam got up and went out into the darkness for his horse. Stormy sat a moment longer, gazing at Holystone, then he, too, left. Holystone was perplexed.

They rode to the herd together, broke away, one riding south, the other west. Now and then a wet cow would look up anxiously and rattle her horns as phantom riders coasted by.

There was the musty odor of cattle, the grunts, half sighs made between cuds, the dark lumpiness of bodies at rest, the white faces. Occasionally a wild one would jump up with two hard thumps on the summer-tightened ground, like a buck deer leaving his bed, give a long, shallow snort of breath and a threatening shake of his head at the man smell. But the night was calm, the animals mostly quiet.

Stormy met Sam on the far side of the holding ground. They murmured a few words and passed on by. The night went like that until just before dawn when even the spooky critters stopped jumping up each time a rider passed. And by then, Cookie was up working where little pinpricks of the previous night's fire glowed anew. He poked, scraped coals against a fresh back log, and sparks exploded against the fish-belly-colored sky. Fifty feet from the wagon a riffling creek sparkled over shiny rocks. Sam and Stormy watched daylight uncover it all over a last cigarette, then rode on in.

The whole crew ate to the accompaniment of Cookie's deviling. "You guys make me sick," he growled. "At the ranch you won't eat bacon, but out here you won't eat beef. There ain't a thin brain between the lot o' you. My pappy used to say riders was freaks. Got no brains at all and what they has got's in the wrong end of their carcasses. I believe it, too. Yes, sir, I believe it. Bacon on the roundups and beef at the ranch." He threw a malevolent glare at the five silent, hunched-over men eating doggedly, picked up a stick of kindling, and banged a wash pan of great size with it. "Another thing . . . see here? See what's lettered on the bottom o' this pan? I mean it and don't any of you forget it." The sign said: *I haul water and you can too.* "Creek's exactly eighty-one steps away, uphill both ways. You don't haul water, you don't eat! See that? I don't give a damn how hard you fellers work, I work just as hard. That sign means what it says. I'm tired o' you sponging whelps washing in my dishwater. You want to be so god-damned clean, wash at the creek or haul water for yourselves. I ain't no man's slave!"

Slim got up and rolled his eyes. Holk Peters kept his face low and averted, shrinking inside for fear Cookie might single him out. Boyishly exuberant, he was also easily embarrassed. Sam Oberlin arose, turned without a word, and headed for the rope corral with his bridle slung over his shoulder. Stormy was the last to leave camp and Cookie's final barb was flung after him. Like the others, Stormy ignored it.

Over by the horses, Holystone made a caustically humorous comment on Cookie and everyone laughed a little. The air cleared and Holk Peters's enthusiasm returned with a rush. He snared out his horse, stooped to grab his saddle, and broke into an old range song about Texas.

> *The devil in hell we're told was chained,*
> *An' a thousand years he there remained.*

*He never complained nor did he groan,*
*But determined to start a hell of his own,*
*Where he could torment the souls of men,*
*Without being chained in a prison pen.*
*So he asked the Lord if he had on hand,*
*Anything left from when he made the land.*

Slim Thatcher bent a pained and outraged look upon the youth, jerked up his latigo, and turned his horse once before mounting. Holk didn't see the foreman's expression of disapproval.

*The Lord said . . . "Yes, I had plenty on hand,*
*But I left it down on the Río Grande.*
*Fact is, Devil, the stuff's so poor,*
*Doubt if y'could use it in hell any more."*
*But the devil went down t'look at the truck,*
*An' said if it come as a gift he was stuck,*
*For after examinin' it careful and well,*
*He figured the place was too dry for hell.*
*So in order t'get it off his hands,*
*The Lord told the devil he'd water the land.*
*'Cause he had some water, rather some dregs,*
*Regular cathartic that smelt like bad eggs,*
*So the deal was closed an' a deed was given,*
*And the Lord rode back to his range in heaven.*
*And the Devil said . . . "I got all that's needed,*
*To make a good hell," and he sure succeeded.*
*He began to put thorns on all of the trees,*
*And he mixed the sand with a million fleas,*
*And scattered tarantulas along the road,*
*Put thorns on the cactus and horns on the toads.*
*He lengthened the horns of the Texas steers,*

*And added some inches to the rabbit's ears.*
*He put a little devil in each bronco steed,*
*And poisoned the feet of the centipede.*
*The rattlesnake bites you, the scorpion stings,*
*The mosquito delights you with buzzing wings.*
*The sand-burr prevails and so do the ants,*
*And Texans who sit need iron in their pants.*

"Holk! *Shut up!*"

Slim Thatcher was sitting his horse, awaiting the others with a screwed-up face, and pointed toward the young cowboy. "Lord! Cookie's a pleasure next to *that!*"

Holk burned a furious red, but he was smiling when he stepped across his mount and Holystone, who had been tapping his foot to Holk's tune, now dragged himself across his saddle and beat a gloved fist on his ragged saddle horn and erupted into a quavering, shrill, and Comanche-like wail, adding another verse:

*The heat in the summer's a hundred and ten,*
*Too hot for the devil and too hot for men.*
*Wild boars roam through the black chaparral,*
*It's a hell of a place he has for hell!*
*Red peppers grow on the banks of the brooks,*
*And Mexicans use it in all they cook.*
*Just dine with a greaser and then you'll shout . . .*
*"I got hell on the inside as well as the out . . . !"*

Holystone finished by throwing his head back and making a wild, thin scream. Slim Thatcher's hair lifted, his scalp prickled. The sound died away and Holystone's Adam's apple bobbed. He gobbled like a turkey. Every Texan knew the sound. It struck an off key in each man's heart. When a wild Comanche gobbled, it meant death, and Holystone's sly old eyes were fully on Slim Thatcher.

Stormy broke the tension with a curse. He whirled and rode away, out toward the holding ground, shaking out a loop with Holystone's rickety echo in his head and Slim Thatcher's growl in its wake. He walked his horse slowly, seeing the wilder of the critters start up here and there.

With big Chihuahua spurs glinting gun-metal blue and silver, Sam Oberlin was parallel to Stormy, sitting motionlessly a safe distance downland. He had a calf loop draped over his shoulder, his unsmiling face tilted a little, pointing toward the herd and away from the sun.

Slim and Holystone rode past. The foreman was ignoring the older man. They broke off, began their circling of the herd, bunching up the grazing strays, pushing them back to the holding ground.

Stormy eased into the herd, wove through it, found a wobbly-legged calf, and began maneuvering it out of the press of bodies. Sam was watching. The calf ran into his soft-whirring loop and set its legs, bawled once, a gurgling sound, jumped high in pure panic. When he came down, there were no hind legs under him. Stormy's throw was neat and precise. The little animal went skidding, bouncing, where Holk waited, Barlow knife balanced high. The boy-man bent over, shoved a front leg through the strangling noose, bent lower, groped, pulled. The knife swooped in. A tiny crown of flesh and hair was flung aside, a spiraling welter of bursting pain shot up into the calf's head. He bawled, eyes bulging, lolling tongue dark with dirt, dried blood, and dust. Holk drew out one testicle, far out, looped the gray, glistening cord, and tugged gently. The cord tore. He did it again. There were only four stingy droplets of blood. The pain receded, became a numbness. Next came the iron and the calf's wild scream was muted by smoke and the iron's greasy hissing sound as it bit down into the living flesh. *MVP.* A quick slash at each ear and the ropes were cast aside.

The day went. Time filtered through acrid smoke from branding. Time quivered high with the cry of dumb-brute anguish. Time punctuated by the rush of a maddened cow toward her tortured calf, turned back by the slamming jolt of a horse and rider, the swirling, whistling slash of a quirt, a romal, down across her sensitive nose.

Time and sweat and blood and out of it all, after three weeks, emerged Slim's tally sheet, five men with muscles mauled stringy-tough, faces burned red-brown, and stiff-legged steer calves humped up in dumb bewilderment and pain beside their mothers.

That last night out there was a prickle of extra warmth in the air. Slim smoked and talked around the bobbing body of his cigarette, his gray, upcurling hair shaggier than ever, his squinted eyes pinched down tighter, his stringy body leaner, more worn, and flat-looking. He told them of the tally and wound it up with an unbelieving headshake.

". . . And not a single, solitary dead one. Not a one. Tie that if you can."

The men murmured and went down into thoughtful silence.

It was very unusual. Holystone alone dared dwell upon it.

"There's signs a feller can go by," he began. "I remember up on the. . . ."

"Yeah," Slim grunted, "up on the something-or-other where you got that stuffed hop toad from the Comanches you pack around wrapped in buckskin. Comanche magic. Medicine bundle. You ignorant old goat, you."

Holystone looked hurt. He seemed to draw into himself. It was obvious to the others that Slim hadn't forgotten that turkey-gobbling incident. Then, when Slim's head was down, his mind mulling over the tally sheet again, and when Stormy's ice-blue eyes lay on Holystone, and Sam's black stare was wet and Indian-looking on the old man's face, Holystone said: "Slim, you're going to see something awful happen to you. Something that'll suck the guts right out of you. I seen it in the cloud shadows a long time ago."

The way he said it, full of quiet conviction, made a hush of strangeness settle over them all for a moment. Even Cookie over by his wagon, muttering, twisted his head, fell silent, and let his dour glance rest on the foreman.

Slim raised only his eyes, looked across the campfire at Holystone, looked as though he might speak, but he didn't. For a moment the chill lingered, and what made it especially eerie for them all was the gentle, sad, and steady breeze that rustled through the dark camp and limped away. There hadn't been a night breeze in weeks.

The freshet touched firmly, softly on Stormy's face. It was a delicate, soft-caressing breeze, pure and faint-scented. Far off a wet cow bellowed repetitively. Her calf answered in a quavering way. The men stirred. Stormy turned toward his bedroll. The others gradually broke the circle. Slim watched Holystone hobble away with a cold glance. It was the last night out.

# CHAPTER FOUR

In the morning the sun was glass-bright and golden, not too warm. Slim Thatcher waited until they had all eaten, then he stood up and deliberately ignored Holystone. His gaze wandered first to Sam, then to Stormy. "We got a hundred and six Big Bs. You boys trail 'em up to Buttrick's. All right?"

Sam nodded. Stormy kept his eyes on the half-breed's face. He knew the general direction of the Big B, but had no idea how to trail cattle up there. Sam evidently knew the way.

Thatcher threw a long glance around the churned, scarred earth. A powerful stench of burning hide, horse sweat, man sweat, dried blood, and—almost the brimstone smell of cursing—was in his nostrils. Flies swarmed low along the ground, feeding greedily on little tufts of hair and curling flesh from the bull calves that had been made steers, on the blobs of black, dried blood.

"Good. You two trail up the Big Bs and the rest of us'll hit for home. See you in a day or so, maybe."

Cookie had the wagon loaded, the team hitched. He had hoorawed the loose stock extra horses on ahead. Holk and Holystone threw the last bedrolls over the wagon's side, forward of the chuck-wagon gate. Slim mounted his horse and stood in the stirrups, squinting far ahead where a thin and lazy streamer of dust showed the route of the loose stock. He settled down again when Holystone yelled everything was ready. His small eyes nearly hidden behind their perpetually squinted lids rested distantly on the crooked, crabbed form. His lips moved. Slim Thatcher hadn't forgotten Holystone's prophecy. It wasn't far back in his mind; it was closer to his consciousness than he'd have admitted to himself.

He looked over where Stormy and Sam were lining out the Big Bs, watched the way they eased them through the valley grass and avoided picking up any straggling MVPs. It was all over until fall and Walter Proctor could hope he'd have as good a crew then as he'd had this spring.

Slim loosened his reins. His horse began to move. More out of habit than anything else he threw up an arm and waved at Stormy and Sam, caught their returned farewells, and rode down past the ruts and gouges where the marking had been done and whistled at Cookie. The team lunged, chain harness rattled, the wagon heaved, groaned, then rolled. Holystone and Holk Peters were riding ahead deep in conversation. Holystone's free hand dipped and swooped in elaborate gestures, aiding his limited vocabulary.

Slim turned once, when they were a mile down the valley. He could see specks where cattle were and off to one side larger specks that were riders, close together, lounging along. The Big B cattle knew where they were going, especially the old cows. Twice a year, spring and fall, they were cut out, pushed back to the Buttrick range.

Sam Oberlin lifted an arm and pointed northeast where a dark height of trees was splayed against an azure-crystal sky.

"Big B," he said.

Stormy remembered the ranch. He was slumped, relaxed. A comfortable slackness was in his face. "Who is Colonel Buttrick?"

"Ex-Rebel," Sam said shortly.

Stormy smiled lazily. All Texas was ex-Rebel. He gazed at Sam. "Aren't you ex-Rebel?" he asked.

The half-breed's face clouded. His eyes grew waspish and a sharp retort lay on his lips, then he shrugged. "That's all past," he said.

"Yeah. That's past. A lot of things're past."

They rode through the whispering grass, warmth lying lightly across their bodies, joints creaking as the heat went in. Relaxation was marrow deep.

The valley widened. The Big B cattle plowed along phlegmatically. Trees drifted up to meet them, a creek had to be forded. In its shallow depths reflections stirred, quivered, clouded over with the passing of the cattle. A big hawk of some kind skimmed overhead in tight circles, effortlessly, and was even with the highest hill on Stormy's left.

Sam made a cigarette, smoked it lolling, hat back, the startling contrast of pale red forehead and dark lower face making his scar look livid and greasy. Eventually the black eyes lay on Stormy.

"You did me a good turn. I don't forget good turns."

Stormy's thin smile came up, wavered, and fell away. He shrugged. "You're a good roper, Sam. Maybe we can pair up again someday."

Sam's eyes stayed on the Texan's face for a long, brooding moment before he spoke again. "Maybe. If I got you figured right, I reckon we might at that."

In his too gentle drawl Stormy said: "How've you got me figured?"

The half-breed drew on his cigarette and gave an honest answer. "I figure it wasn't no mistake when you come riding into Marais Valley."

Stormy considered this. He also considered the hard, fierce face of Sam Oberlin, and a suspicion grew. "If you were right, Sam, what would you think of it?"

Again, bluntly, Sam answered. "I'd think it might be a

damned good thing. Marais Valley's as good a hide-out as Texas has got."

"You think I'm hiding?"

Sam punched out his cigarette on the saddle horn, shredded it through his fingers. "No harm if you are," he said carefully.

Stormy's smile came up. "Would I be the only one hiding, Sam, if what you think is true?"

Sam scowled a little. "No, I reckon not. Are you running?"

"Yeah, are you?"

"Sort of." Sam looked up. "I been here a year now," he said.

Stormy twisted sideways in his saddle. "All right. That's two of us. Now what?" It warmed him inwardly, this dark secret they were sharing.

Sam looked out over the broad, fat backs of the cattle where they wound among the willows in a thicket, emerged past it onto an almost limitless plain of short, strong grass. "The Mex border's about thirty-eight miles south of here," he said.

Stormy followed the half-breed's gaze and understood. Fat cattle—Mex border. It backed up in his craw contemptuously. Colville and other places had spoiled him for stingy profits and long chances. Sam Oberlin was a beetle-browed novice, a half-blood tough, nothing more. Stormy shook his head.

Sam saw the motion. His dark scowl returned. "You don't like it?"

"Naw. For one thing the cattle're too fat. You'd kill half of them pushing them hard."

"The other half'd bring good money."

"Not enough," Stormy said, scorn showing. "When I take a chance, it's for bigger profits. The risk is the same both ways, so take the one that's most worthwhile."

"Like what, then?"

Stormy looked at the sinking sun, the blurring outline of far-away hills, the soft-stepping purple coloring of dying day marching down from the ramparts. "I don't know," he said. "I haven't been around here long enough yet to have more than an idea. Anyway, I haven't been thinking along those lines lately. Give me a little time."

They rode in silence until the soft, velvety gloom surrounded them. Much later, Sam grunted his answer. "I'll wait," he said. "Make it good when you come up with something, though. I'm running out of patience, sitting around playing poker every damned night and mucking moss out of water holes every cussed day." The dark eyes lifted unseeingly over the dark-bobbing backs of cattle. "Sitting, waiting, makes my guts crawl being cooped up in this valley all the time, listening to Slim and that imbecile Holk Peters, and old Holystone. Sometimes I could jump the bunch of them to stir up some life."

Stormy leaned forward, peering into the lowering distance. "I see a light up yonder a ways."

Sam's hot glare swung with banked fires. "Big B," he said shortly. "I'll lope ahead and open the gates. We won't have to push 'em from now on. They know the way in by heart."

Sam was lifting his reins when Stormy spoke, his face a pale outline in the warm night light. "Relax, Sam. I think there's something in this valley that'll make us both rich."

Sam's scar shone dully when he said: "Yeah, I've thought of that. Old Proctor's got money cached around. Buttrick, too, more'n likely."

Stormy wagged his head again. "Not that, either. Something bigger, Sam."

The half-breed reined up, puzzled and irritated. "What the hell are you talking about, anyway?"

"Bigger'n a gun job. What would we get out of robbing them? Maybe three, four thousand dollars."

"Well, what's wrong with that?"

Stormy reined up, also. They sat there, looking at one another while the cattle shuffled on through the darkness. "I've made all that kind of money I want to make," Stormy said. "The next chance I take'll be for life, Sam."

Sam's jaw muscles rippled. The shadows filled in and overran the hollows under his eyes. The scar was rusty wet in the pale moonlight. "What in the hell are you talking about?" he said harshly.

Stormy jiggled the reins. His horse moved ahead slowly. "Let me think it out first," he said.

Sam rode in humped-up silence for a ways, then he kicked out his MVP horse and loped widely around the cattle toward the lamplight that glowed steadily up ahead. From a long way off he helloed the ranch. Stormy listened to the click of horns and puckered up his eyes unconsciously. Sam Oberlin—Marais Valley. *Take your time,* he told himself. *There's something here. The biggest risk of all. It's in the air, in the grass, in the gun-metal eyes of a full-bodied girl. . . .*

Up ahead lanterns bobbed. Men's voices raised in the darkness went down the night to him. He kept the drag moving, closing up until he was near enough to make out angles and corners of corrals. Shaggy shapes of men moved under the lanterns. The one on horseback would be Sam. He swung his quirt lazily at a high-headed heifer that was lagging. She gave a grunt, a big jump, landed hard up against other animals.

Cattle went plodding by, their passing marked by a whispering rub of bodies, a rattle of horns. A gate creaked closed after the last of them, and Stormy sat still, studying the men under the lanterns. He picked out Colonel Buttrick easily, lean, sinewy, assured. A wide-shouldered man beside him would be his son, perhaps, or maybe his foreman, although he looked pretty young for that responsibility.

Three riders were chousing the cattle and talking among themselves as they went down the outer corral fence, peering in at the cattle. The lean, gray-headed man approached Stormy with a half genial, half testy expression. He threw up his hand.

"Colonel Buttrick. You a new MVP man?"

Stormy leaned, grasped the dry, brittle fingers, and dropped them. "Yeah, Stormy Merrill."

"I see. Well. . . ." The colonel turned, jerked his head. The wide-shouldered man came up. "This is my foreman, Carus Smith. Carus . . . Stormy Merrill . . . MVP."

Smith's face was wide-mouthed, square, the eyes deeply set under thick brown eyebrows. He smiled and shook. "Proud to know you. We're obliged you fellers brought the cattle up. We'll start working this end of the valley next week. Fetch yours down then."

Sam dismounted and made a cigarette, and a tall, willowy rider walked up close to him. He had black hair and pale blue eyes. His mouth was quirked into a half self-conscious, half reckless look.

"Howdy, Sam."

"Howdy, Deefy."

"Got tobacco?"

"Yeah."

They lit up and smoked.

Colonel Buttrick took the tally from Stormy and said Stormy and Sam should go to the kitchen and eat, spend the night at the bunkhouse. Sam heard. His dark eyes went past Deefy Hunt to Stormy, stayed there while Stormy accepted, then dropped away sullenly. Sam said nothing.

Big B's kitchen was cleaner than MVP's. The cook was a Mexican woman of unbelievable girth and tough good nature. Sam threw her a grunt and dropped down at the table, pushed back his hat, and waited. Stormy smiled at the woman, the pull of womankind coming up in him. She returned his look with a dazzling smile and Sam noted dourly who got the best slabs of meat, the largest slice of crab-apple pie. It amused him in a bleak way.

After they had eaten, Colonel Buttrick came into the kitchen. With him was Carus Smith, bareheaded, his brown hair tightly curled, dull-looking in the yellow lamplight. Buttrick was smoking a crooked cheroot, his lean, saddle-bowed legs encased in high boots and faded blue trousers. His features were sharp, predatory, alert. Stormy felt his vitality, his inherent toughness, and the cold strength of mind that came into the room with him. He waited, understanding that in Colonel Buttrick stood an adversary equal to any a man might meet in a long lifetime. It made his antagonism and caution stir together. This was no fat, slovenly, whiskey-smelling Walter Proctor.

The colonel's eyes flashed over Sam's dark face and stopped on Stormy's. It was a tribute, in a way, that Sam didn't seem to notice. He went right on eating.

"When you get back, Merrill, ask Walt if he'll sell that horse you're riding? My daughter's taken a fancy to it."

Stormy nodded gently. "That's not an MVP horse," he said. "It's mine."

"Oh." Buttrick showed no surprise, and Stormy knew suddenly that the colonel had used that opener as an approach to trade. Inwardly Stormy drew off, studying the man. He wasn't just brittle-hard; he was calculatingly hard as well. A hard man to think past. "What'll you take for him."

"He's not for sale."

"Any horse is for sale, Merrill."

Stormy's glance darkened. "Not that one," he said.

Colonel Buttrick regarded him silently for a moment. "Sleep on it," he said. "In the morning I'll show you fifty horses just as good."

Stormy pushed his plate away and reached for his tobacco sack. "All right," he said, and held the paper motionless, watching Carus Smith and Colonel Buttrick leave the kitchen.

Sam looked up suddenly. "You'll get a good swap out of him. He'll make you an offer you can't turn down. When he wants something, he pays for it."

Stormy finished the cigarette and lit it. He watched the Mexican woman thumping a huge batter of bread dough. In Spanish he said: "I think he is a Texan." Among Mexicans it was an uncomplimentary way of hinting that a man was unscrupulous.

The woman turned with sly amusement in her smile. She winked at him. Also in Spanish she said: "Sometimes I think he is a devil. His daughter is just like him."

"So? And where is his wife?"

The dark eyes rolled. "Ahh. She is on a long trip into the States somewhere. Every second year she goes like that. A formidable distance, friend."

Stormy digested that. With a twinkle he said: "Perhaps your husband is also away on a formidable trip, as well?"

The woman's eyes sparkled. There was hungry wistfulness in their depths. "Twenty years ago, friend, who knows. Now. . . ." An expressive hand moved swiftly up and down the gross body. "If I *had* a husband, what you hint at would still be only a politeness."

Sam's dark face was pressed down in concentration, trying to catch a word now and then. His success was indicated when he arose in disgust, took his plates to the sink, dumped them in, and stalked out of the kitchen.

Stormy stood up, hat far back, a coil of damp hair tumbling a little below the brim. He also put away his dishes, then he reached over and laid his hand lightly on the woman's shoulder, squeezed, and left by the back door.

Outside, Sam was waiting by a tangled bed of geraniums. He threw a disgusted look at Stormy. "Don't you care where you sleep?" he said.

Stormy looked out over the yard where light lay in puddles diluted by moonlight, soft and mellow. He said: "It won't hurt to make a friend up here, Sam."

He left Sam in the shadows and walked down to the corral where their horses were, leaned on the poles listening to the animals chewing hay, snuffling at the dust in it, and their gray, sweaty bodies glowing in the watery opalescence of the night. Cigarette smoke drifted up and around his hat brim. In an adjoining corral were more horses. He moved farther down the darkness to see them. There were good animals in the bunch. He could make them out easily, sleek, well cared for, quality horses. Several were better appearing than his own horse, and that made him wonder why Buttrick's daughter wanted his animal, which in turn made him ponder. So far, from what he'd seen of Buttrick, if he *had* a weak spot, a blindness, it might be the girl.

He threw down the cigarette, stomped it dead, and stepped up to straddle the corral poles. Perched up there like a big owl, he picked out the horses he might trade for, if he traded at all. Traded to satisfy a spoiled girl. He heard no sound behind him because the horses were moving, blowing their noses, and squealing at one another around the worn-smooth pole feeders.

"See anything you like?"

He twisted and looked down. She was smiling up at him. Moon glow splashed upon her ash-blonde hair, shimmered over it like water, and the confident smile she wore marred the perfection of her features a little. She was like her father in a way; he could see it in the dull light. Lean and willowy, small-breasted, wasp-waisted, long-legged, erect. Her eyes were greenish in color, her mouth long, soft, full above a round chin and the Buttrick jaw. Confidence emanated from her. Tantalizing arrogance. He forgot the trade, the horses, and the old cruel hotness swam behind his belt buckle. The boldness was up in his eyes when she said it again.

"See anything you like?"

"I reckon I do," he said softly, then more softly: "I see something I like right well."

She didn't shy away from the tone, but came closer, leaned on the corral, and gazed in at the horses, the smile not quite so open perhaps, the green eyes straight ahead.

"Then trade for it, cowboy," she said coolly. There was a hard sound to her voice, no breathlessness. It yanked him up short. This was no girl burning red with a shared secret. This one knew her weapons and her world.

He slid down off the corral and stood beside her. She was a foot shorter and sixty-five pounds lighter than he was. Straight and supple, soft-curved and magnetic. He turned slowly and looked back at the horses like she was doing, retreating a little, mentally stalling, going back in his mind in search of surer footing. "What's one horse when you've got the pick of so many?"

She laughed. It was a trilling, rippling sound against the somber night. "I collect horses, cowboy, like some people collect pictures."

"Do you always get the ones you want?"

She looked up at him sideways and a hot wave of color beat into his face. "Always . . . cowboy."

Stung by her condescension, he said: "I've got a name."

"I know. Stormy Merrill. I've got one, too," she added slyly, waiting, triumphant, while he groped inwardly, knew she'd outmatched him on names, and grew angry.

"You don't know it, do you? It's Antonia. Toni." The green eyes came fully around, mocked him. "Put a price on him, Stormy."

His breathing was shallow. First the father and now the daughter. They laughed at him secretly, mocked him, handled him offhandedly. For the moment he hated Toni Buttrick with a genuine and intense dislike. There was an answer to her question, but he would not give it, green eyes, wide mouth, or not.

"He's not for sale."

He was turning away. She reached out, caught his arm, and stopped him. The smile on her face made him itch to slap it away. "I used the wrong approach, didn't I, Texan? Look . . . see that palomino mare . . . ?"

"I wouldn't be caught dead riding a mare."

"How about that white-stockinged black horse, then? He's four years old and broke for anything. One of the best horses on the ranch."

The horse was easily worth twice what Stormy's animal was worth. He looked around at her and spoke gruffly. "What's wrong with you, lady? What's so wonderful about my horse?"

She swung him completely around with the hand that still lay on his upper arm. The fingers closed down, nails dug into his flesh. "I just want him. That's enough, isn't it?"

He stiffened under the tingling pain, under the brassy assurance, the arrogance of her smile. There was cruelty in his steady stare. Without answering he reached for her, brought her in against him, and kissed her angrily, hotly, wanting to hurt her.

She shivered once, lost her erectness, and a wild flame flooded through him when her mouth responded to his own, the long width of it tightening, holding his lips and meeting pressure with hurting pressure.

Blood roared in his ears, in his mind. This was more than a girl with a hungry secret who stood off in shame afterward. This was a meeting of wills, a battle of lips, desires, hardness. Then she was struggling against him, fighting clear. He released her, heard the rasping pant of her breath in the stillness, saw the emerald of her eyes glowing with wicked fire, heard the erratic explosion of her breathing.

"Well!" She put both hands on her face, staring at him. "Well!" Then she laughed in that trilling way and let her hands fall. "Great God! 'Way down here in Texas, at that." The green eyes kindled, grew brilliantly wondering. "Where did you learn to kiss like that, Texan?"

He showed the high banner of cruelty in his gaze when he answered. "I've been practicing . . . waiting for you."

The green eyes threw it back at him with irony. "And gallantry, too. Virginia has nothing on Texas now." She moved one hand, quickly, like she thought he was going to run. "Stormy . . . quit MVP. Come to work for Big B."

For a moment he was like a statue, staring hard at her, then he bent, searched the ground until he found a sharp pebble, straightened with it cupped in his fist in front of her, opened his hand like he'd done with the first girl he'd met in Marais Valley, and let the stone fall. "Why, you need a new toy?"

He turned on his heel, and walked toward the soft glow of the bunkhouse lights.

# CHAPTER FIVE

The Texan rode back the next morning beside Sam Oberlin with a livid memory carved in the soft parts behind his eyes. Sam, never inconsequentially talkative, said nothing for miles, then he studied the white-stockinged black horse and grunted approval. "You come out 'way ahead on that swap. I told you he'd make you trade."

"Sam, tell me what you know about the girl?"

The dark eyes swept upward. "Girl? Oh, you mean his daughter? Not a hell of a lot. She went to school in Virginia. I've heard that a dozen times. Been back couple months. Pretty in a skinny sort of way, isn't she?"

"Yeah."

"I like Jerry better. Filled out more . . . more meat on her bones."

"Jerry?"

"Geraldine Proctor. You've seen her around the ranch."

"I didn't know her name. Yeah, I know what you mean."

They rode leisurely, nooned at a gravelly creek where cattle watered, where horn flies and animal scent lay heavily, then pushed on down the land with the sun's brightness slanting against them. A blue jay paced them for a while, its strident cry becoming harsh and annoying through persistence. They arrived back at MVP after dark.

Slim Thatcher was up at Proctor's when they angled into the yard. Sam was tired. He ate at the kitchen, then went to his bunk, kicked off his boots, hung his gun and hat upon nails, and turned in. Stormy sat down to the poker game with Holk Peters and Holystone. They welcomed him with smiles only, crouching over their cards.

Stormy lost. He couldn't keep his mind on the game. He still heard the trilling laugh, saw the hot green fire in her eyes, and felt the tightening of her mouth over his. He lost $7 and went outside until the closeness of the bunkhouse, its smells, were flushed out of his head. Making a cigarette, he looked up at the silvery moon, as lonely as a god, riding across a sky that held thin streamers of iridescent clouds.

Spurs rang softly from the direction of the house. He turned and watched Slim cross the yard. When he called the foreman's name, Thatcher veered off from the bunkhouse and came up beside him.

"Made it all right?"

"Yeah. Carus Smith said they were going to start working stock up there next week, maybe, and they'd bring down any MVPs."

"That's good," Slim said casually. "Any other news from up there?"

"None that I heard. I traded off my horse up there, though."

Thatcher peered at him. "How come?"

"Got a better one and the colonel's daughter wanted mine." He shook ash off his cigarette. "When she makes up her mind . . . that's it."

Slim fished around for his tobacco sack. "Yeah, I remember her from when she was a beanpole with pigtails. Used to throw fits and the colonel'd get redder'n a beet and give her whatever she wanted to shut her up. It used to make my palm itch to blister her bottom." He lit and exhaled. "I haven't seen her in four, five years." His gaze grew quizzical. "What's she like now?"

"About the same as when you knew her, from what you say,

only now she's grown up."

The squinted eyes drifted past Stormy's face, northward. They looked reminiscently for a moment, then cleared and lifted to the high sky. "Sure a pretty night, isn't it?"

"Sure is. I got cleaned out in the poker game."

Slim smiled. "Holk's getting downright good. Say, Mister Proctor wants the wagon to go out to Fort Burnett tomorrow, and we always send a couple of men with it. One to tool the wagon, the other to help load at the other end. How about you and Holystone?"

A coldness ran in under Stormy's heart. Fort Burnett— people—lawmen. He erupted a gust of smoke, dropped his cigarette, and carefully decapitated it with a spur rowel. "I was hoping there'd be some riding to do around here so's I could get acquainted with my new horse."

"Ride him to Burnett," Slim said matter-of-factly. "You don't have to ride the wagon if you'd rather take your horse along."

"All right."

Slim nodded, and crossed the yard toward the bunkhouse. Stormy watched him go and thought that Thatcher walked like a man whose problems, if any, were very small ones.

The next morning Holystone had the team hitched right after breakfast. He scrambled up and chirped at Stormy from the high seat, faded old eyes dancing. There was an improvised cover over the wagon seat made from the bows and cloth of a buggy top. Stormy blinked at it, saw Holystone's excited grin in its shade, and went after his stocking-legged horse.

He had saddled, was leading the animal from the cool interior of the barn when he saw her, and stopped stockstill. She was being helped up beside Holystone by Slim Thatcher. Her father was standing close, scowling at some lists in his hand. She didn't see him and he knew it was purposely that way.

Standing there, gazing at her from the dark maw of the barn, his mind drew an automatic comparison. Toni Buttrick's slimness, her green fire. Jerry Proctor's smoldering eyes, softly closed mouth, heavy, sensual, lying composed without pressure, the more mature fullness of her, the high and arched prominence of eyebrows, the gun-metal, thunderstorm grayness of her eyes.

He mounted the black horse and turned his head, looking northward up the valley. Summer sunlight shone down in bright yellow brilliance. It was shredded gold through the trees and dappled across the yard. His fist tightened on the reins and a savage dagger of thought bored deeply into his mind. He could have this one, he and God knew that. The other one—the green-eyed witch—neither he nor God could say.

He heard Walter Proctor's sluggish monotone and turned a little to gaze at the big man. Proctor seemed tired, unkempt, even when he was explaining what Holystone was to do in Fort Burnett by tapping the written instructions he held. The voice droned on. Stormy heard words without heeding them and involuntarily he sought her face again under the buggy top. It was composed, eyes looking straight ahead, ignoring him so totally he felt they would all notice it, but apparently none did.

Finally Holystone sang out and the wagon creaked. Slim Thatcher strolled over beside Stormy. "See that the old fool stays a little sober, will you? He lives through the whole year for this trip. Usually gets a hide full if he isn't watched close. Don't let him embarrass Jerry."

Bold blue eyes dropped to Slim's face. "I didn't know a woman was going along," Stormy said.

"Well, she 'most always does. It's her only outing. You know how women are. . . ."

Stormy shook out the reins, the black horse stepped out. He didn't know that Slim's geniality was dying, that an odd expression was on the foreman's face, following him, that Thatcher's hand hung in the air because Stormy had ridden off without a word, a sign of any kind.

The wagon took the spidery old road and wound over it like something blind being led in clumsy, groping slowness. Stormy rode in the rear, far enough back to avoid most of the curling dust, and through the leaves tumbled filigree patterns of burnished sunlight.

When they came to the place where he'd first met her, deep and secret-looking in its mantle of shadows, it was as though an invisible finger touched each of them lightly upon the heart. He could see her back straighten. Could also see the dew-shiny blackness of her hair sway with the rhythm of the wagon. He let the full-coursing storm of memory run its limit, then he made a cigarette and smoked, lost in a moist, fluted corridor of thought.

He could have her, with her went half of Marais Valley. The thought plagued him. But half wasn't enough. The boldness showed in his eyes. A man should own it all. But how? He shook his head in despair, but all the same a thrilling pre-taste of triumph was there. He had no idea how to get the other half, yet a man should own all the valley, not just half of it.

Daylight jumped up at him, flooded over both him and the black horse, fell away rearward. He inhaled deeply on the cigarette, watching her strong, supple back, sitting up there beside old Holystone. He could own half the valley by marrying a woman. One of two women. One or the other of them, the gray-black eyed one or the green-eyed one, it didn't matter. He smiled and his face looked to be laughing heartily in total silence. There ought to be a way to marry *both*. And risk? There wouldn't be any. The biggest gamble he had ever imagined, for the most gain—and no risk. All of Marais Valley starting with half, and no posse after him for the biggest steal he had ever conceived. The smile stayed strong. Plan big enough and you become above the law. The question, then, was which woman?

He studied Jerry's back all afternoon, until the long, narrow shadows blurred it and the obsidian sheen of her hair was obscured, mantled so that it blended with the twilight. With the coolness, the valley fragrance, and the total peacefulness of the long day, his woman hunger grew and grew, to be shattered only when Holystone pulled the team out into an old glade that had seen a night camp of north-bound travelers, and called out to the horses as he kicked hard on the foot brake.

Stormy dismounted, made it a point to ignore her just as she had ignored him all day. He gathered wood for Holystone's cooking fire in thoughtful preoccupation, keeping his back to her later, when he drew out his own and Holystone's bedrolls from the wagon. She would sleep off the ground in the wagon; they would sleep a discreet distance away. He brought water from the nearby creek and hunkered, back to her, when he hobbled the horses.

Holystone hummed a whining chant, made a little fire with a pinpointed flame that came up under the frying pan, and cooked meat and potatoes. In honor of Jerry's presence—and because he was quivering with anticipation of Fort Burnett—he whipped up sourdough biscuits lighter than a feather.

They ate mostly in silence. Holystone, hugging his secret eagerness close, suspected nothing, and as the evening closed down, thickened, Stormy gazed steadily into space as though miles away in thought. And she began to steal glances at him; shame and discomfort staining her cheeks, eyes cloudy.

Holystone chirped an inane conversation, mostly one-sided. Going to Burnett was the milestone of each living year for him. His spirit soared, wouldn't be depressed by anything, was blind and self-centered. It erected a barrier around him as high as the sky and as thick as armor. He noticed nothing, heard nothing, felt nothing beyond the breathlessness of his own anticipation.

Eventually there was a white magnificence to the heavens and the sad, silvery moon was large, tilted, slumped patiently amid the thousands of its progeny, raffish, little nictitating things that glowed and faded, glowed and faded.

Later Holystone sat back, shoulders against a fore wheel of the wagon, eyes broodingly pinioned by the fading coals of the fire, lost in silent reverie. For Stormy the sudden silence was an uncomfortable time full of dark discord and emotion. He lay back upon the grass, a long, strong silhouette rounded upon the earth.

Gazing upward, with shadows moving in the background of his eyes, he heard Holystone stir, grunt to his feet, and shuffle softly in his rickety way to the far side of the wagon. A premonition stirred and Stormy listened, then stood up. Over the far side of the wagon box he could distinguish Holystone's tilted-back head. He stood immobile and a slowly curving smile lifted the corners of his mouth. Let him, the old devil. Let him drink it all, if he wanted to. Stormy lay back down, staring upward. There was a greenish tint to the sky seen through the trees leaves nearby. Green fire, cold, arrogant.

He moved, swung his gaze away so that the leaf taint was gone and only a shiny blackness remained, a shadowy gunmetal color that reminded him of arched eyebrows. Half the valley. . . . Let the crippled old fool get drunk. He thought ironically of the trust, casually given, in Slim Thatcher's face, back at the ranch.

There were waves of awareness shimmering invisibly in the night. He could feel them, lying still looking upward, and, as the hours tolled by and she made no move to retire, but remained humped over by the dying fire, he knew.

Holystone came around to the fire and squatted, trying to cope with the growing restlessness that gnawed from within, an unappeased appetite that a trickle only aroused for more. Then he got up and went around the wagon again, and Stormy's smile lay faintly upon his features, ghostly white teeth showing, reflecting pale moonlight like new ice.

Seven times Holystone made the pilgrimage. The eighth time he didn't return and Stormy heard a faint, keening chant that Holystone crooned to himself as he poked his tarp around, head east, feet west, Indian style, unrolled the bedding, and fell atop it, breathing heavily until he coughed.

The night was warm. Moonlight broke over the water of a little creek close by making white caps where real ones had never existed. A cat bird called drowsily, and Stormy raised up on one elbow, turned with the boldness bright in his eyes, and gazed at her. She was holding her knees with both arms. The fullness of her shown faintly. He made no sound, and yet she turned her head slowly, looked at him. There was something solid and vibrant in the night between them.

The night was in her eyes. They were black, wet, bottomless. He got up, went over, and stood above her. She looked down into the graying ashes, watched them stir with dying movement, heard the soft moan of his shell belt, the solid thump on the ground when he sank down beside her. A shiver passed through her.

Past her he could see trees by the creek, hung with a ghostly patina of silver, up closer, the way her hair threw back the blaze of moon softly, in curves of hushed light. He saw something else—two silvered marks on her cheeks where tears had passed—and they stirred him only with the hard knowledge of his triumph to be.

In his imagination, the green fire atrophied, died out, and the girl beside him with her nearness, her night-heightened beauty, desirability, answered the day-long question in his mind without struggle, without thought. He would take the lower end of Marais Valley; it would come to him with Jerry Proctor.

He reached out, touched her, felt her stiffen, let his hand lie lightly. "What's the matter, Jerry, scared?"

"Nothing." She whispered it.

A brightness was in his eyes. His future was clear to him. No more running, no more posses. Half of Marais Valley now, half later, until he figured how to get the other half. His fingers tightened on her. The heat of his palm went through to her flesh and burned there. So easy! There was a growth of something hard in his throat, a burning deep within him, a blind rushing of woman hunger. He pulled her down to him. She didn't resist, but lay limply, passively on the grass, looking up into his face, and he could see the still, black depths of her gaze through a sheen of moisture.

"Why were you crying, Jerry?"

"I wasn't . . . not really crying."

He leaned closer, tracing out the soft heaviness of her mouth with his glance, the faint beat of pulse in her throat. She didn't speak above a whisper when she spoke at all.

"Why are you doing this, Stormy? To see if you can?"

He shook his head. "Because I want to and because you want me to."

Her features lay pale, agitated. "Like the time you kissed me. . . ."

He bent low, feeling the off-key roll of her heart in his own chest, kissed her. She pulled back from his hurting pressure and clung to his mouth with a strange and haunting tenderness. It was an altogether new sensation to him. A gentle, all-encompassing, and tireless sensation that engulfed a man, drowned him, and held him forever. He could feel it closing over him and struggled against it. Pulling himself up, he propped his head on one arm and stayed that way, motionless.

Below him, Jerry's eyes were closed. He was conscious of the wet softness of her lashes, the way her mouth lay like always, closed and heavy, without pressure. She was a beautiful thing. It shook him momentarily. Beautiful, yes, half of Marais Valley, the most beautiful valley he'd ever seen.

He raised one hand and blotted away a single tear that lay sideways across her cheek. Touching the dark profusion of her hair, he saw the burnished silver of moon glow run before his hand. He put his fingers deeper into it, curled them into talons, and pulled, gently at first, then harder, more cruelly. Lifted her head off the ground and crushed his mouth down against hers.

That was when the fire burst through, exploding in a wild tumult, blinding them both with the savage, feline ferocity. She returned his kiss with an abandoned passion far exceeding anything he was capable of.

When they parted, his hand shook a little as he let her head down upon the crushed grass. Her eyes were wide, shiny, and her heavy mouth was no longer composed, closed, but lay parted, the teeth showing through, the flesh bruised, scarlet. He could hear the pounding rhythm in his head, the crashing cymbals that came from his blood.

"Jerry. . . ."

Her eyes drank in the hard boldness of his face, the handsomeness with its vestiges of ruthlessness. She didn't move and might have been dead or asleep the full length of her body except for the barely seen quivering of her nostrils, the whispering rush of her breath. "Why, Stormy? You don't love me."

He was a moment answering. "Have I said that?"

"It's . . . so wrong."

"No," he said quietly, "not wrong." His right arm was tingling from supporting his weight so long and he ignored it. "That first time on the road, Jerry, when your horse went lame. . . ."

"I kept the little stone."

"That didn't just happen, Jerry. Why were you there when I came riding from three hundred miles away and met you? Why weren't you somewhere else . . . so I never would have met you? It was supposed to be that way."

She stirred. "I don't know. But it's not right . . . like this."

He shook his head. The coiled mass of his hair, too long, rank, and handsome under the soft light, shimmered. "Anything we do is right."

"Without love?"

"Love? Could you do this without love? Neither could I."

She held his eyes with a glowing, haunting hope that was sadder, more knowing and understanding than believing. Very, very softly in a whisper she said: "That isn't so, Stormy."

The arm was paining him now with an angry urgency. He had to shift position. "It is for me," he said.

She rolled her head sideways, looked over where the creek was. The night was still then. Holystone, on the far side of the wagon muttered thickly, incoherently in his sleep, choked, coughed, moved sluggishly, and let out a long whistling groan.

"Jerry?"

She rolled her head back. The sadness spread down from her eyes, to her cheeks, settled lower, on her mouth, and he saw it, was aroused by it, bent low, and kissed her. That time she threw both arms around his neck, held him tightly.

# CHAPTER SIX

Holystone awoke with a caked taste of corral dust in his mouth and a frothy, insatiable thirst he quenched again and again at the creek. He sluiced out his gullet, gargled, choked, swore, and spat the water out, hobbled back where the fire had been, squatted to stir up the dusty coals.

When his eyes fell upon the grass across from the ashes, he frowned, studied it, then stood up and craned his neck to see where the horses were. They were bellied full of grass and drowsing nose-to-tail near some willows. They hadn't trampled and bedded that grass, then. What in tarnation had? The sun bounced off the baked earth and smote him painfully in the eyes. He hunkered down, mumbled growlingly to himself, and poked at the fire. To hell with the grass; the sun hurt his eyes.

He tugged his hat lower, peered from under it at the mound of a man where Stormy lay dead to the world under his tarp. Holystone grunted. *Funny, Stormy was usually first one up when they were out . . . like on the roundup. Well, let him sleep . . . no hurry especially.*

But half an hour later when breakfast was fried and Stormy still lay unmoving, like a stone, Holystone got to his feet, went over by the bedroll, nudged it with his toe, and frowned moistly when two blue eyes came abruptly open and stared up at him like frosted agates.

"C'mon, dammit. We got to make Burnett *sometime* today."

Holystone went past the wagon, thumping its sides with his

fist, but not looking up. His mind fastened upon this new irritation and was able to forget a little of his personal headache. Back by the fire, sullen-looking, hunched over, eyes nearly closed against the sun, he called surlily: "Let's eat!"

Stormy went far up the creek, stripped to the hide, and took a chilly bath, re-dressed, and went back to the glade where a tangy scent of food made him aware of a ravishing hunger.

She was there.

He halted short, back in the willows, looking at her. The tangled mass of dark hair was caught up and held like he'd once imagined it should be, and his thin smile came up. He'd told her about that; how he'd pictured her in the house the night of the storm.

Quite suddenly she turned, saw him staring from the willows. A dark flood of color ran into her face, but she smiled with her level gaze soft. He hadn't seen her smile; it twisted something inside him. He pushed past the willows, went over and sank down close beside her. Without another look or a word he speared fried meat and began to eat.

Holystone's eyes watered profusely. He had to dash away the unwelcome tears with the back of one hand. Inwardly he groaned over the way he felt, kept his head down, but the sunlight leaped off the ground and scratched at his eyeballs.

Jerry laughed in a deep, husky way full of warmth. It startled Stormy. He looked at her, saw how her nose crinkled, the way her throat undulated, the clear goldenness of her flesh. She pointed at Holystone. Stormy looked and understood. Holystone knew they were laughing at him, thought he knew why, too, because they knew what he'd done to make his head ache, his eyes water, but he didn't know that their deepest, secret mirth lay in the fact that they shared something else at his expense. Their own private secret, hugging it close, protecting it.

Holystone suspected nothing until the wagon was packed, the team harnessed, and Stormy was standing beside his stocking-legged black horse, then Jerry, who Holystone had known since early adolescence, did a strange thing. She reached over, took the reins out of Stormy's fingers, and handed them to Holystone, bent her face close, and said: "Holystone, you ride, will you? Let Stormy drive the wagon."

Holystone looked from one to the other, saw the still eyes, the expectant expressions, crinkled up his forehead, and looked suspiciously at the black horse.

"You two up t'something? This critter got a quirk in him and y'want to see me get throwed sky high?"

Stormy said no, there wasn't a buck or a fault in the black horse anywhere. He said it after he'd handed Jerry up into the wagon and had his foot on the fore-wheel hub.

Holystone stood uncertainly, perplexed. He made no move to mount Stormy's horse until the foot brake was kicked off and the team leaned against the wagon's weight and began moving. Then he turned, cocked a puzzled eye at the patient black horse, got aboard, took a deep seat, kept his eyes on the little black ears, snugged up the reins, and booted the beast out. Nothing happened.

Holystone rode for forty minutes before his perplexity was resolved, then, coming around a shady bend in the road where he had a good view of the wagon, he saw Stormy loop the lines, turn his head, and meet Jerry's profile in a long, clinging kiss.

Holystone sputtered, gasped, was horrified. He didn't know what to say, do, or think. He rode dumbly, saw her move closer, lay that wealth of beautiful hair on Stormy's shoulder. He saw Stormy's thick shoulders slant against her, his arm feel its way around her waist, and he said to the black horse: "Great God! What'll Mister Proctor say!"

They swung northerly in a loose, wandering way, left the

eroded roadway, and Holystone followed, grim-lipped, moist-eyed, and miserable. They topped out over a long swale, dipped between hillocks, buttes, summer-dry, rustling, ridden by a shimmering scorching heat, and finally came out onto a great vacant plain, enormous and naked. There, Jerry pointed to a distant, ugly, and brown-looking growth that was Fort Burnett.

Stormy thought back to Marais Valley, its hilled-in peaceful-ness, its solitude and isolation, its sturdy trees and dark green floor with the blue overhead. He thought he had never seen a finer country; he never would. By comparison the Fort Burnett country was bleak, dead.

The town wasn't much. It straggled and was bedraggled. Dust inches deep muffled the horses' footfalls. The buildings were old, mostly adobe with an occasional wooden house or false front. The people seemed to be mostly Indians and Mexicans. Freighters in thick, heavy boots, with huge half circles of sweat at their armpits stood or strolled. The sun was bright. It spanked the town, threw long shadows where it couldn't reach, and dogs, slab-sided, crafty-looking, abounded.

Stormy's gaze grew sharp, dry, bit into everything he saw, but mostly into the faces. Behind his shirt a troubled heart beat; in his mind was a shrill little warning that rattled around. Texas was big, but Colville wasn't too far off, either, not to the kind of men he saw on the hard walks of Fort Burnett. Freighters, express riders, scouts, Indians, cattlemen, Mexicans, all sorts of restless people whose eyes had looked at sundown from a hundred different towns.

Jerry sat primly erect, the very soul of respectability—well, almost—the touching legs were concealed by the voluminous skirt.

Behind the wagon, Holystone's dark and brooding counte-nance made it plain to anyone who cared to see that something outrageous had happened. Something had cut down deeply into the core of his sense of responsibility and it showed through the sweat sheen of his old face.

"Over there, Stormy . . . that's the mercantile."

Stormy laid the wagon in close to the hard walk, set the brake, and looped the lines. Casual glances swept over them, went past. Some were arrested by the handsome black horse Holystone was tying to a post behind the wagon. Hardly any dipped to the old rider himself.

Stormy got down, went up to the horse's heads, made them fast, and flipped the check rein off, then walked to Jerry's side of the vehicle. She looked down into his face; a wistful hopefulness was plain in her eyes. He held up his hand, her fingers lay across his palm, cool, firm. Their glance didn't break until she was standing beside him, then he turned as Holystone stumped up with a wintery look.

"Before we get the stuff for the ranch, Holystone, take a little walk with us."

"Where?" Holystone sniffed, suspicion and antagonism in his face. "I want t'tell you two something. . . ."

But they were walking north, wending their way almost hurriedly through the passers-by. Holystone had to swallow his words, and hurry, crab-like, so as not to lose them.

They found the house with its black-lettered sign: *Justice of the Peace.*

Holystone froze, warped legs stiff, head thrown forward. He began shaking his head like a fly-maddened bull before Jerry or Stormy even turned to see if he was following.

"Damned if I will! Cussed and damned and double-damned if I will!"

Stormy's expression underwent a subtle change. His eyes fastened themselves upon the older man, his mouth grew wider, thinner. But it was Jerry who went back, laid a hand on Holystone's arm, bent a little, and put her face close to his, and spoke through the foggy, sour smell of whiskey breath, low and quietly and with urgency.

"Holystone, it's all right. There aren't any ministers in the valley. You understand, don't you?"

"Your paw'll skin me alive. Jerry girl . . . what's come *over* you? Lord A'mighty . . . I've knowed you since you was that high. I never seen you act like this before. You don't even know . . . why, good Lord, girl . . . you two only been together this trip. You just *can't* act up like this."

Her fingers found his sleeve, tightened on his arm, felt the stringy old muscles beneath the shirt. "Please, Holystone. You've *got* to. . . ."

The moist old eyes blurred. "Girl, your paw'll kill me. He'll just up and. . . ."

"Now he won't, either. Holystone, he won't say a word."

"He don't know. You don't know what he'll do. Listen, Jerry . . . think, girl."

Holystone held out. He argued and stamped his foot and rolled his sore eyes, but in the end he went in with them, moved by one cold sentence from Stormy that was bitter and humiliating and true.

"Hell, Holystone. For a dollar I can hire any of these saddle-bums to stand up as witness. This is an honor and Jerry wants you to have it."

But Holystone trembled all through the ceremony and the final words, sepulcher-sounding, solemn and quiet with terrible finality, made his mouth alkali-dry, his chest full of a rattling fear. Fear, as big, as terrifying as any fear he had ever known, dwelt in him, was all through him, and stayed, undiminishing.

On the way back to the mercantile he thought no more of Fort Burnett and what it stood for in his narrow life. The plans to sneak away and get owl-eyed drunk were gone. All he was positive of was that somehow, some way, Stormy Merrill had betrayed Holystone's trust in her and he, in turn, had betrayed Walter Proctor's trust. He groaned aloud.

At the mercantile Stormy laid a hand lightly, briefly on Holystone's shoulder. "You've got the lists," he said placatingly, half smiling, eyes like dark turquoise. "Take care of things. We'll be back."

They left him alone, more lonely than he'd ever felt before. He watched them walk away, arms touching, the sway of her thigh in step with the bold man beside her.

The afternoon sun was setting. A thought and a shiver passed over Holystone where he stood stupidly watching them disappear. *No! He can't! Proctor'll kill him!* His hand with the crumpled list in it contracted spasmodically. The mercantile proprietor came out onto the hard walk, stared, then moved closer.

"Hey, MVP, are you sick? Here . . . give me the list. You'd best go see. . . ."

Holystone relinquished the list and started walking with his crooked gait, string-halt muscles jerking him along like a fiddler crab. Walking. . . .

The sun sank low, slanted fiery lines down across Texas, set the heavens ablaze with billowing, blood-red riot and from an upstairs window of The Freighters & Travelers Rest, Jerry leaned upon a cigarette-scarred window sill and looked out at it.

Stormy was beside her, back a foot or so. The long, curved sweep of her back, the tumbling wonder of her hair let loose, falling in rich thickness, the fullness of her, leaning that way, and the good, gentle lines of jaw, of throat. . . . He reached for her and she came around passively sweeping up against him.

"Stormy . . . Stormy."

He smiled. There was a strong upcurving of the hard mouth, a deep hungering in his eyes. "You don't have to whisper any more, we're married." The sound of it, the realization of it meant nothing to him. He said it again, louder. "Married."

"I know." Her voice rose a little but was still low, softly low. "Oh, Stormy . . . if we've made a mistake. . . ."

Her arms crept up around his neck, pulled his head down until her mouth lay inches below his, waiting, showing hunger that burned no longer ashamed, no longer in secret.

"We haven't made any mistake."

There was a hard core of realism in his tone. Almost harshness. Tilted back, close, her face was blurred. Outside a knife-edged voice, clear as a bell, thin and deadly rose up to them, was heard but unheeded.

"You old fool, watch where you're walking. . . ."

# CHAPTER SEVEN

The road back was strange. Holystone rode the black horse in brooding silence. His lips were blue, his cheeks ashen. He'd had his drunk—a good one, the only one he'd had in twenty years with a reason, for he'd never been able to find the two that night. Stormy tooled the wagon and Jerry leaned back looking down the brilliant land toward home. Her face was serene with an unearthly gentleness, the unblinking gaze with a strong expression of fulfillment.

They made their one-night stop and all were moodily silent. Holystone wouldn't look at either of them. They retired early and were up early, continuing their journey. Once they saw some riders in the middle distance, westward, and Stormy watched them intently until Jerry spoke.

"Big B. They've probably started their roundup."

His expression softened. "Sure," he said. "I'd forgotten."

She drew his head around and held him with a steady stare. "Stormy . . . have I told you you're a handsome man?"

He smiled indulgently at her. "It isn't that, Jerry. You've been locked away down in this valley all your life. I came along, a stranger, someone you weren't used to, hadn't seen before. . . ."

A shadow passed over her face. After a moment she said: "You don't really believe that, do you?"

He still smiled at her, but didn't answer. Shrugging, he looked out ahead, over the team's heads toward the familiar twists in the road.

"Because if you do, Stormy," she said, "then you don't believe we're really in love."

A sharpness flashed briefly in his eyes. Without turning, he said: "Sure, I'm in love, Jerry. I've known a few women, but you haven't known many men. I know what I got, but you don't."

She reached up with one hand and ran a finger down along the curve of his jaw, up over the hardness of his chin to his lips, felt their elastic toughness, on up his cheek to his eyes and beyond, up where his carelessly worn hat curled upward with a graceful sweep. She removed the hat, put it in her lap, and ran her fingers through his hair.

"I know what I've got, Stormy, and it's all I'll ever want."

He said nothing. The back of his neck felt hot and prickly from her touch.

Behind them Holystone's sunken eyes were miserable, fixed on the wagon's seat. His body swayed dejectedly to the black horse's gait.

They rolled into the MVP yard when darkness lay like a blanket over everything. Stormy got down and helped Jerry alight. When she turned away, he caught her arms, held her, and spoke aside to Holystone. "Put up the team, will you?"

They crossed the yard together. He heard the bunkhouse door open and knew long silhouettes were lying forward in the doorway, but didn't turn. Jerry felt for his fingers. Her hand was damp, warm. At the gallery near the big old rosebush she stopped and turned toward him, released his hand, and said: "Wait."

He waited. Made a cigarette, lit it, and saw glowing light when a lamp came on inside the house. His heart beat in a sturdy, sharp way, smoke trickled from his nose. The murmur of voices came, then a man's voice exploded shortly, subsided, stopped, then resumed more slowly. Moments later she was coming through the door, Walter Proctor, sleep-tousled, behind her, big enough to block out the light momentarily. Stormy's right arm hung at his side, the left held his cigarette. His blue eyes, wide and watchful, were direct.

"My husband, Dad," she said.

Walter Proctor was like a pillar. He offered no hand, made no sound.

Jerry turned so that she was facing her father from beside Stormy. The silence grew, thickened. She nudged Stormy; he slowly raised his arm, put out his hand.

Proctor's eyes in the rose-scented gloom were hard to see, but the deepest sort of anguish showed clearly in his features. With tight lips he took Stormy's hand, gripped it in a big fist, and dropped it. He slumped, round shoulders going lower. "Well . . . ," he said, and stopped, seemed to struggle inwardly, and made a humorless quirk with his mouth. "I'm sort of out of breath." The sound of his own voice seemed to rally him. He looked at Jerry. "You could have told me, Jerry. It's an old family tradition, but we usually have our weddings at home."

"Dad . . . I'm sorry." Her voice low, but her eyes weren't.

He let his gaze drift back to Stormy. It was an ill-looking gaze and Stormy was uncomfortable under it. He still said nothing.

Jerry said: "We could have a wedding celebration, Dad."

The big man nodded heavily. "Yes, we'll have that, anyway."

And that was all that was said. He turned and went back into the house. Stormy felt relieved, but Jerry's stillness, the way she watched her father walk away, showed sorrow.

Stormy turned her, led her deeper into the darkness down the gallery by the big rosebush, placed her so that the ragged limbs made a fretwork for the lamplight to struggle through behind her.

She shook her head slightly. "I was terribly selfish, Stormy."

"He'll get over it."

She looked at him oddly. "He's always been so kind to me. It

71

wasn't very considerate."

"Maybe the party'll make him feel better."

She was silent a moment. "Stormy, do you have parents?"

He shook his head. "No kinsmen at all." His mouth closed firmly over those four words. She heard the warning ring in them and understood.

"It makes a difference, though, Stormy."

"What do you mean?"

"Someday you'll know. Later, when you're a parent."

For some reason that startled him. His eyes widened a little but he didn't speak.

She half turned, looked out past the rosebush across the yard. "Stormy, what do you want out of life?"

"Want?" he said. "You, that's all."

"But don't you want a big family?" She turned to look at him.

His breath came in a rush and made a soft sound. He recovered slowly. "Later, honey," he said quickly.

She moved, went up against him, tilted her head, and held his eyes with her own. "Maybe, Stormy," she said enigmatically. He didn't understand what she meant and didn't try to very hard. The blood was singing in his ears again. He reached for her, held her tightly, and bent his head to kiss her.

"Good night, Stormy."

He watched her go into the house and stood in the scented shadows until the fire in his blood died out, then he turned and looked out across the yard. Over at the bunkhouse lamplight spilled in a shimmering, golden way from two tiny windows, made an orange paleness against the rising moon. High in the sycamore near the barn an owl made soft, repetitive calls to himself. A long way off a horse neighed and overhead a fierce arcing of flame marked the scratch of a meteor upon the face of eternity. Its tail left a lurid streak of green fire across the purple panoply; some of it stayed in Stormy's eyes, faint, but green and remembering. He made a sound in his throat and moved off the gallery, crossed the yard, and entered the bunkhouse. The room was filled with a weighty silence. Holystone was slumped over at the poker table. Holk Peters was leaning, head propped on his hands, just staring from his bunk. Slim Thatcher's expression was cold and unnaturally stiff. The only gaze that hung on Stormy's face with any familiarity was the dark one of Sam Oberlin. In Sam's expression was saturnine amusement.

Without speaking to any of them, Stormy tossed aside his boots, hung up his hat and gun, lay back on his bunk, and stared up at the slats of the bunk above him.

Slim Thatcher said: "Congratulations."

Softly Sam Oberlin chuckled.

# CHAPTER EIGHT

It took time for Stormy to establish a footing with Walter Proctor but he did it. Circumstances made such a thing necessary. Jerry was alternately wistful and sad until her two men unbent toward one another at least a little. It was difficult for her father. He and Slim Thatcher held a painful, one-sided conversation one day when Stormy and Sam were out on the sagebrush plain southward, mucking out water holes. The result was that Jerry supervised the rehabilitation of one wing of the old house into private quarters for the newlyweds. Even Cookie was pressed into service. The house was given a thorough cleaning, something that had been neglected too long. The parlor was made to sparkle, and through all the turmoil Jerry's flushed face and sparkling eyes haunted the minds of her father and Slim Thatcher.

Down where the sun was the hottest, sweating under the still heat of a shade tree, Sam and Stormy sprawled on the limp grass beside a water hole they'd cleaned, and smoked. Sam was speaking in a hard, dour way.

"Foreman, Stormy? He'll have to do it now."

Stormy looked into the pool of water. "That'll be your job, Sam."

"Oh?" The black eyes glowed. "And what'll you be, part owner?"

The blue eyes lifted, grew still and challenging. "Yes." Sam smoked a while. "What'll you do with Slim? I reckon you've noticed he don't like you."

"I don't give a damn what he likes. He can stay as a rider or he can push on."

Sam rolled over, propped his head up, and flicked sweat off his chin. "All right. I'll go along with everything you've done so far . . . everything you've said . . . but just what the hell's in the back of your mind and where do I fit in? Remember, you said you'd tell me when you got things figured out."

"I've got them sort of figured out, Sam. Like this. Why Rustle MVP cattle when I can own them? Why risk using a gun when a wedding ring'll do the same job without bullets? Does that make sense?"

Sam pursed his lips and nodded. "I reckon," he said, "but what about Proctor?"

"What about him? Hell, he don't run MVP, it runs itself and he just straggles along."

"Uhn-huh," Sam assented, then looked up and sighed. "You know, I never did get you figured out."

"Don't try."

Sam squinted placidly at the burning sky seen through limpid tree leaves. "All right," he said, smoked a moment before he spoke again. "You want to tell me the rest of it?"

"Rest of what?"

"Hell. You're no more the kind to marry a ranch and set back than I am. You got to have something ahead of you. What else you got under your hat?"

Stormy tossed dirt into the clear water, watched it sink lazily, catch sunlight, and flicker. "Not yet, Sam," he said.

"But there's more, isn't there?"

"Yes, there's more."

"I thought so." Sam struggled up, threw a quick glance at the sun. "It's all right with me," he said. "You make me foreman soon's you can and I'll string along and keep my eyes open, mouth shut." He dusted off his jeans. "We'd better be getting back . . . be sundown directly."

They rode together in a vacuum of silence. Shadows slipped out around them, grew long and heavy. When they topped out over the high plain, below which lay the hidden greenery of Marais Valley, Sam pulled up, dropped his reins, and sat there humped over, gazing downward. A pre-twilight haze overhung the lowland. The faintest spindrift of Oakwood smoke scented the air.

"If a feller could settle down, Marais Valley'd be about the best place I know of." He looked around at Stormy. "Sure tucked away."

"Yeah. Y'know, Sam, we can pick this place for a long time. What I've done is legal . . . strictly legal."

"Sure, but I don't understand how we'll get rich from this."

"You blind?" Stormy asked. "When I'm running MVP, the ones who sell cattle will be you and me."

"Yeah? How about Proctor?"

Stormy shook out his reins irritably. "Let me worry about Proctor. Right now he's the least of my worries. I got half an empire to get yet." He led the way down into the valley.

At the ranch yard, Holystone saw them come down the lane, cross to the barn and unhorse. He watched, thoughtful speculation on his face. Slim Thatcher straightened up nearby, looked out of the sparkling window that Cookie had cleaned, squinted eyes steady, mouth pulled flat.

Jerry heard Stormy's spurs on the gallery and hurried to meet him. She caught his arm, swept him down the gallery past the rosebush, around the lower end where a blank space of wall hid them. He looked at her with a tiny scowl.

"What's wrong?"

"Nothing. I brought your things to the house. We've got our own place now." She leaned upon the wall, hands behind her.

"It's a surprise for you, Stormy."

The tenseness went out of him. He bent from the waist, brushed his mouth across her lips, caught the fragrance of her, and leaned farther, kissed her roughly.

"What'd your paw say?"

"Say? He was the one who put the boys to work in the house." She put a hand on his chest, holding him off. "And Holystone's going over to Big B and invite them to the celebration."

"*Humm,* when'll it be?"

"Day after tomorrow." She cocked her head at him. "That's all right, isn't it?"

He smiled. "It is with me, sure. Those are a wife's end of things."

Inwardly the change in his status pleased him; outwardly he remained the same. The awkwardness that had never disappeared when he and Walter Proctor were together began to fade after their first supper in the main house. At the wedding celebration, it remained only in their eyes. In all other ways, outwardly, they accepted one another.

When the Big B came riding in, Deefy Hunt, perched atop the seat of a spring wagon they'd brought, was singing scratchily and lustily. MVP heard the racket five minutes before they saw the entourage.

It was evening with a long draft of coolness lying low in the shadow lands of the valley. The MVP riders were turned out in their best and for the first time since the Fort Burnett trip, Holystone was his noisy old self. He hobbled around in a fog of his own whiskey-laden making.

They ate, the bride opened gifts and looked radiant in a tight-bodiced, long, flaring-skirted dress of great age. The heavy mouth was curved and parted. Slim Thatcher, from across the large parlor, felt a knife turn in his innards. Holk Peters leaned against the wall, watery-kneed, breathing shallowly. Only Sam

Oberlin's admiration for Jerry was slight. He had a strong contempt for womankind regardless of beauty. Walter Proctor interested him far more than Stormy's wife.

Deefy Hunt and Holystone made irregular but persistent excursions to the darkened bunkhouse. Colonel Buttrick finally sent Carus Smith after Hunt with a grim admonition. Stormy sat through the noise and excitement with a faint, fixed smile on his face. He wasn't as uncomfortable as he'd imagined he would be, and across from him a pair of mocking green eyes baited him unmercifully.

Elmer Travis and Bob Thorne of Big B went out to the wagon, brought back a fiddle and a guitar, and tuned them up on the gallery. Holk Peters, at the sound of music, straightened off the wall and went outside. From a pocket he brought forth a mouth organ. The three of them worked up a sort of harmony that increased as they played and Deefy Hunt, angular, thin, began a grotesque dance with old Holystone to everyone's vast amusement and howls, until Hunt was framed in and chilled by the dampening stare of Colonel Buttrick. Even Walter Proctor laughed. He motioned to Slim Thatcher.

"Let's move the furniture back, Slim."

The dancing began in earnest then. The musicians sat along the north wall, perspiring, adding their rhythm to the stamping of booted feet. Stormy had the first dance. Toni Buttrick, light, supple, curled against Carus Smith. Colonel Buttrick and Walter Proctor watched through a swirl of cigar smoke. The colonel shook his head at the noise and edged toward the door. Proctor followed him. Together, they were like a wasp and a bumblebee.

Outside, the night echoed with sound and Colonel Buttrick groped for a chair, found instead a bench, sat down on it, and looked up at his host. "Funny thing about 'em," he said without any preliminaries. "You can plan and hope, but when the chips are down they'll do as they damned well please."

Proctor settled against a gallery upright by the rosebush. He looked over the colonel's head at the wall and nodded without speaking.

Buttrick said: "Toni now. I got Carus and made him foreman, practically raised him, Walt. She doesn't pay any more attention to him than if he wasn't around . . . unless she wants him to do something." The colonel's darting eyes lingered on his cigar. "Now what? I've made a good cowman out of him. He's good-looking enough for any woman. Steady, too." He made a hard chuckle. "I've got a son-in-law without benefit of marriage. Son-in-law without a wife. Dammit, Walt, what makes them different, anyway?"

"Maybe there's someone in Virginia."

Buttrick shook his head savagely. "No. She laughed when I asked her that. She said Virginians aren't Texans and she wouldn't have one for a slave."

Walter Proctor shifted his weight, crossed his arms across his chest. He looked blue around the eyes, sag-muscled, ill. He said: "I'd sort of figured on Jerry doing differently, but, if she's happy, why then I've got no call to fuss, I reckon."

The sharp eyes swept up, dug into Proctor's face. "Know anything about him, Walt?"

"Just that he's a top man with stock . . . and a Texan."

Buttrick's thin face split into a hatchet smile. "Well, that used to be enough, didn't it? Are you going to make him foreman?"

Proctor looked down thoughtfully. "I've got a good foreman, Colonel. Jerry's after me to sort of let Stormy take over a little." The troubled, ill-looking eyes lifted to the colonel's face. "Hell, it'll all be hers someday, anyway, won't it?"

Buttrick gazed across the yard, involuntarily frowned at the scatterings of discarded things he saw in the moonlight. A fastidious man himself, this was Walter Proctor's one trait he didn't approve of, this slovenliness. "I guess so," he said vaguely, and stirred on the bench. "You sent a wagon to Burnett, didn't you?"

Proctor gazed at him ironically. "Yes."

"Any worthwhile news come back?"

Now Walter Proctor smiled. "Well, my daughter got married up there," he said. "That was news enough for me."

"Oh, that's when it happened, is it?" They both smiled, Proctor a little ruefully. Colonel Buttrick got up, rammed his hands into his pockets, and looked idly through the window at the dancers.

Walter Proctor pushed off the upright. "Come on around back, Colonel. I've got some good bourbon in the office." They went down the gallery together.

Inside, Holystone, head thrown back, was chanting one of his wordless songs to the rhythm if not the tune of the music, and Stormy was whirling Toni Buttrick. She laughed up into his face, when they swung close, and spoke: "You're a disappointment. I thought you were smarter than you are." Then she swung out again, green eyes showing enough contempt to sting him. He jerked her back up close, crushed her to him, and said: "You didn't think anything. You don't think, you run by instinct."

The green fire burned. "You think so, do you?" She pushed him away, then swooped past. "Where's the black horse?"

He blinked. "In the corral, why?"

"I'm going out to look at him in a few minutes. When they start laying out the food." She broke away from him when the music stopped and said something to Carus Smith, then laughed, and the Big B foreman's face shone down at her with flushed pleasure.

Stormy turned his back on dancing. His heart was thudding with a foreboding. He saw Sam Oberlin leaning in a corner, smoking, and went over by him.

"She's a wild-acting rig, sometimes," Sam said.

"Who?" He bent to the task of fashioning a cigarette.

"Toni Buttrick . . . who else?"

Stormy lit up and looked across the room where Carus Smith was hovering over the green-eyed girl. His thoughts were dour and strangely restless. "Yeah," he grunted. "Damn her, anyway."

Sam turned, looked, then made a bleak grin. "She want the black horse back, now?"

Stormy didn't answer. His wife swept by, reached out with a brush of fingers, a flash of her eyes, and disappeared in the direction of the kitchen.

Sam crushed out his cigarette and deposited it in the cuff of his pants. "Well . . . they're putting up the sideboards. I'd better go help." He gazed at Stormy a moment. "You better go outside and dry off, you're redder'n a chile pepper."

# Chapter Nine

Stormy went out onto the gallery. The night was glowing with soft whiteness. He looked up at the moon and it made some of his irritation wither to see it as he'd thought it would look when shining over Marais Valley, that first time he'd reined up and seen the hidden range below him.

He walked west along the front of the house, cut across the yard, went behind the bunkhouse, and swung far around the barn to the corral where his black horse was. The animal was eating placidly. It raised its head to look at him, then returned to eating.

His heart was pumping; the cigarette tasted bitter. He stepped on it, leaned on the poles, and waited. *Risk,* he thought. This could put the fat in the fire. It was crazy meeting her like this. If MVP didn't see them, Big B might. His irritation roused up anew. What was wrong with the damned woman, baiting him to meet her like this? The boldness crushed down his misgivings. He gazed steadily at the horse. She had a right to come down there to see the animal, almost as much right as he had. It was plausible. He turned away, leaned on the corral, and gazed into the shadows, saw her coming, a slim willow of a woman whose movements, whose outline and closeness made a tingling power course through him, a tantalizing recklessness. She stood for the other half of Marais Valley.

"I didn't think you'd do it, Texas," she said, coming closer.

Scorn showed. "Why not?"

"Thought you'd be afraid to." She cocked her head at him, green eyes showing a dull, sly fire.

She could stir him with her bluntness, her teasing arrogance, her long mouth and upsweeping gaze that kindled fire out along his nerves, in his blood.

Softly he said: "Lady, there isn't a thing in this world I fear."

"I like that, Stormy. Virginians aren't like that. They're gentlemen and I don't like gentlemen."

"Don't you?" he said harshly, and swept her up to him with one arm, using his free hand to force her head back so that she was arched against him. He kissed her. She moved and inside his heart he bled, felt raw and strangled with passion and pride. He let her go. She didn't step back or put up her hands as she'd done before, just stared at him, flushed.

"Lord. . . ." It was so low he hardly heard it. In an instant the mood had passed; she was her teasing, arrogant self again, half laughing, half taunting. The silver light illumined her odd beauty, its litheness, suppleness, its peculiar and exotic wickedness. "Why did you marry her, Stormy? Why?"

He didn't answer. Conscious of her swift-rising bosom, of their primitive rapport, he kept silent. She reached for his arm, hurt it with digging fingernails.

"Why?"

"Because I wanted to. Why else?"

Ahhhhh," she said throatily. "You damned fool. I could have done everything for you she's doing . . . only better."

A pale smile touched his mouth. He thought of the valley and nodded. "I reckon you could've, at that."

"Then why didn't you give me the chance?"

His smile lingered, mocked her. "I will, Toni. I'll give you the same chance."

Anger exploded in her eyes. She spoke swiftly, the breath rushing outward around the words. "No, you won't, Texan. Not now. You know me and you know her . . . damn you . . . you'll have plenty of nights to think about it, regret being in such a hurry." She turned, balanced on one small foot.

He caught her, swung her back toward him roughly, felt the cable-like toughness of her muscles tighten, forced her arms behind her, and lowered his head, met her mouth, the long, tightening mouth.

Their kiss was savage and raw. The blood in his head pounded, surged through him like green fire, then he let her go and smiled coldly down at her.

"Yes, I will, Toni. Listen to me. I'm going to hunt strays tomorrow morning over near Cap-Rock Spring. I'll be there no later'n noon. You come."

"Not on your life, I won't."

"You come, Toni. I want to talk to you."

She made a hard laugh. "Talk to me?"

His smile faded, the bold eyes lay on her intently. "Yes, I want to talk to you . . . talk!"

After she'd gone, he smoked a cigarette. The sound of voices, of chinaware, of loud laughter and calls came mutedly from over by the house. He turned his back to it and gazed at the handsome black horse. His mind was leached dry, his body sagged. He smoked, thinking of the savage passion, the hard bluntness of her. The black horse ate unconcernedly. Tantalizingly he thought of the Buttrick half of the big valley, of the measureless wealth one man would control if he owned both halves. Well, he had one half. No, not yet. He stirred, moved his feet. He'd have Jerry suggest to her father that he give her the ranch, let Stormy run it. Proctor could retire then, spend all his time drinking. He spat, crushed out the cigarette. Who did Proctor think he kidded, making out he wasn't well. Stormy knew an inveterate drunkard when he saw one. Jerry would get MVP because she was her father's only child. Fine. There was still the Buttrick half. Toni, sure, but how? The colonel's weakness was his daughter. Stormy's mouth quirked ironically. And Toni had a weakness, too—Stormy. There lay the solution, then. He didn't know how he'd work it, but there it was. Being married to Jerry was an obstacle—or was it? He thought back to Toni's words, her actions, and thought: *No, Toni wasn't bound by social ethics. She'd bend with the wind.*

He turned and gazed over at the house lights while the riddle revolved lazily in his mind. She'd be at the spring, he didn't doubt.

"Stormy?"

It was a man's voice, sudden and heavy. He didn't move off the corral poles, feeling a shaft of hot guilt. "Yeah? Who is it?"

"Me. Walt."

The big man's rolling bulk hove into sight through the shadows. He was bareheaded and unarmed. He came on with a slow, ponderous tread. "Get too much for you?"

There was nothing but Proctor's slow geniality in the voice. Stormy relaxed. "Got a little noisy," he said.

Walter Proctor came up and shoved big, fisted hands into his pockets. He had a faint, self-conscious smile on his face. "Yeah. Y'know, it's odd how women are. They like solitude, but when they throw a party the more racket and confusion, the better." Walter chuckled softly. "A man gets used to peacefulness and never wants it interrupted." He studied the younger man's predatory face, leaned a little against the corral, looked over it somberly at the black horse. "Well, Stormy, I got something to say." He paused watching the black horse. "Jerry's got a husband." Another pause. "Well, it stacks up about like this. MVP will be her's one of these days. She might as well have it now."

Stormy's heart beat sturdily, unhurried and strong. The same thought ran through his mind that had occupied it on his first day in the valley. This was too easy.

Walter Proctor's profile swung, his big face looked head-on at the younger man. "Jerry and you and me'll be pardners in MVP. Does that sound all right?"

"It's up to her," Stormy said, making his voice casual to the point of indifference.

The big man's apathy vanished. He looked closer. "You two weren't thinking of leaving, were you?" An urgency was coming into his voice. "She loves it here. You'll get so's you'll never want to leave, too. The valley does that to people. It grows on them. Now, if you two went away. . . ."

Stormy felt for his tobacco sack without feeling any need for a cigarette at all. "I like it here fine, Walt. We haven't talked about leaving." Walt was anxious; he was afraid Stormy might take his daughter away. He lit the cigarette, savoring this knowledge.

Proctor watched him in shadowy silence. Watched the cigarette curl to life and give off smoke. "Well, you're a pardner in MVP from now on, Stormy. We'll keep it a family outfit."

"Thanks, Walt."

They walked back to the house together without speaking, the warm night lying across their shoulders, the shadows parting for them. Colonel Buttrick was smoking one of his crooked cheroots on the gallery. He watched them approach and there was an envious, troubled expression on his face.

Walter Proctor veered off at sight of the colonel, went over by the big rosebush, and eased down on the gallery railing. The two older men watched Stormy enter the house without speaking.

Inside, a wave of roiled heat struck him. He saw Jerry dancing with Slim Thatcher whose old-fashioned grace was plated with small gallantries. Watching, he thought that Slim, for all he was ten years older than Jerry, seemed to compliment her in some elusive, indefinable way.

Sam Oberlin emerged from the throng, walked to the sideboard nearby, put some food on a plate, and strolled over beside Stormy. Toni was dancing with Carus Smith. She looked at him once from across the room, a long, cold look, then she smiled up at the Big B foreman. Smith's face broke into a grateful expression. It reminded Stormy of the look a lost dog gives when someone throws it a piece of meat.

Sam said: "Walk a little softly, Stormy."

He looked at Sam, recognized the ironic light in his eyes. "What're you talking about?"

"Nothing," Sam said, eating and watching the dancers. "Maybe everybody isn't as suspicious as I am, but you'd be a damn' fool to take the chance. I missed you, and I missed *her* at the same time. Quickest way in the world for a man to spoil something real promising is to get women mixed up in it."

Stormy's anger flared hot. He said nothing and Sam went on eating.

Hours later the gaiety dragged and people lost their enthusiasm. Jerry, quick to sense the lag, brought the party to an end and saw that the guests were bedded down. When the house was quiet she found Stormy out on the gallery by the rosebush, came up behind him, and touched his hand. He turned. She looked fresh and lovely in the dying light.

"Did you enjoy it, Stormy?"

"Very much. Danced enough to make my feet sore."

She looked at him, then away. Softly she said: "Slim had most of my dances."

He understood, almost carelessly took her in his arms. There was an easier way with Jerry. He kissed her, held her close, and rocked her a little. She melted. With his mouth against her ear, pressed to the Stygian luster of her hair, he said: "Let's get some sleep."

"All right." She was moving in his embrace.

"Jerry, your dad came down to the corral where I was smoking. We talked about the ranch."

"Yes, I know. He came to me, asked me where you were." A warning ticked in his mind. "And?"

"I'd seen you go outside. He went looking for you."

"It got kind of hot and noisy in there," he said slowly. "I wanted a smoke."

"I imagined that's what it was. What did he say to you?"

"That the three of us would run MVP."

"That's what he told me. He said he'd make you a partner." She leaned back and looked at him. "Do you want that, Stormy?"

He groped for the right word, couldn't find it, and frowned. "I reckon so, Jerry."

They walked into the house to their room. She took down her hair before a square mirror. He struggled out of boots that his feet had swollen into.

"Dad'll leave the running of the place up to you. He isn't well. Hasn't been well for several years."

Stormy looked up. "Oh? What's wrong with him?"

"His heart. I suppose it never was really healthy, but after my mother died he got worse." She turned away from the mirror, watched him fight the boots, red-eyed, grim-mouthed. "It'll all be up to you. Is it . . . too much? I mean, would you rather not have the responsibility, Stormy?"

He sighed and tossed the last boot aside. "I can cut the mustard, Jerry," he said. "Don't worry, I'm not scared of responsibility."

Her gray-black eyes rested on him. "What I meant was . . . would you rather go away, somewhere, the two of us?"

He stood up, puzzled, seeing the strange thoughtfulness in

her face. "Go away? No, I don't want to leave Marais Valley. Why?"

She reached for a hairbrush and turned her back to him. "Oh, I just thought you might want to. Might want to start out on your own . . . or something like that. After all, I don't know you well enough to know what you think, Stormy."

He stared back at her, at the long sweep of loosened hair, then grunted. "No matter where we went it wouldn't be like the valley."

"No," she agreed softly. "I'd rather stay. . . ."

"We stay," he said.

There weren't many hours left to the night and dawn came with its customary liquid-copper, swift-running brilliance, and hush. The shadows fell back beneath the trees to re-group and lie sullenly until evening came again to release them.

Cookie beat his triangle belatedly, but with unusual good humor, making rhythm on it. His look chilled only when Stormy came in early, ate, and left, went out the back way, around the house where people were stirring, down to the barn, and began to fork feed to the livestock.

He was sitting in the shade by the sycamore tree when Slim Thatcher came strolling, making his after-breakfast cigarette. There was an unmistakable purposefulness to Slim's gait. With a nod he dropped down beside Stormy, inhaled, exhaled, and looked up the wide sweep of valley. "Quite a party," he said.

"Yeah."

"It's been a long time since there's been one at MVP," Slim said, keeping his glance on the land, the sere, rising hills, and the pure turquoise sky. "They had one up at Big B when Toni came home . . . only I couldn't go."

Stormy looked at the foreman's profile. Was there meaning in the words? He decided not. Slim was a cowboy, nothing more. Stormy leaned back and closed his eyes. "I could sleep for a week," he said.

"I reckon." Slim paused, listening to the clamor over at the house where MVP and Big B were reliving the dance over their breakfast. "It'd been better if we'd had another three or four girls. That way, when one left it wouldn't have made any difference."

Stormy's eyes opened wide, grew still. They were on Slim's face, stayed there. He said nothing. The little warning in his mind was trilling steadily now.

Slim arose, stomped on his cigarette, and looked past the barn at the corrals where the horses were. "You feed the stock?" he asked casually.

"Yeah."

Slim nodded without looking at Stormy. "I expect there won't be much to do today." He walked away, down the yard toward the corrals, and Stormy's eyes followed him.

# CHAPTER TEN

Carus Smith came out with Holystone hobbling beside him. Behind them was Deefy Hunt and Sam Oberlin. Holk Peters and Elmer Travis of Big B were chiding Bob Thorne, also of Big B, about his ability as a dancer. Stormy stayed in the languorous shade, watching them cross the yard. When they were close enough to see him, he got to his feet. Carus Smith's boyish face split into a grin.

"Getting up this morning was the hardest thing I've done in a year," he said.

Stormy smiled. "Me, too. Think I'll just hide out today and sleep."

Holystone snorted. "That's the trouble with young fellers nowadays," he said. "When I was a young buck, we'd dance all night and work cattle all day and chase Indians for supper appetite."

Deefy Hunt looked at Holystone from beneath his hat brim. In a dry, lazy way he said: "Shouldn't 'a chased 'em afoot, Holystone. Look what it done to your legs."

Holk Peters broke into peals of laughter. Holystone shot him a long, menacing look that brought smiles to the other faces, then stamped off toward the corral where Slim was leaning, the sun burning through his shirt, warming, relaxing tired muscles.

The men split up, some going into the barn, others wandering down where Slim and Holystone were. Sam Oberlin eased into the shade beside Stormy. His hat was tugged forward, eyes squinted.

"We got a day to kill, Stormy."

"You have," Stormy, said. "I've got a little chore to take care of." He scowled toward the aimlessly wandering men. "What'll they do today . . . you got any idea?"

"Laze around, I reckon, why?"

"Those people've got more eyes'n a Comanche . . . especially Thatcher. I want you to keep them from riding over by Cap-Rock Spring."

The dark eyes grew speculative. "All right, only I don't expect there'll be much done in the way of work around here today. What you got up your sleeve?"

"Going for a ride, Sam. Don't worry about it."

Sam looked down at the shaded ground and shrugged. "Suits me. I'll get a poker game going, maybe. That ought to hold most of them."

Stormy whiled away the hours down by the barn. There was more coolness there. There was also solitude. Once he was interrupted by Colonel Buttrick. He was soaping his saddle when the Big B owner came in out of the sun blast, blinked, and came closer.

" 'Morning, Stormy. Hotter'n blue blazes out there."

"Sure is, Colonel."

Buttrick watched the long, firm strokes as Stormy worked. "Are you still satisfied with our trade?"

"Plenty satisfied, Colonel, only I can't figure out why you did it."

Buttrick's thin lips parted mirthlessly. "You will someday, Stormy. You will someday." The brittle eyes clung to Stormy's face. "Walter talk to you about the ranch yet?"

Stormy didn't look up because there was annoyance in his face. "Yes," he said shortly, "we talked a little last night. Why?"

Buttrick heard the irritation and ignored it. "It's the opportunity of a lifetime, Stormy. When I was your age, things like that didn't happen. A young feller could marry ten owners' daughters and he'd still have five years' apprenticeship to serve out."

Something the colonel had said amused Stormy. "I don't know as I'd care to marry ten owners' daughters," he said lightly. "I reckon one woman at a time's enough."

The colonel nodded. "Well, it'll make you, boy. MVP's a big responsibility. You'll either measure up or you won't." The clear eyes lay steadily on Stormy's face. "I see the strength in your face, all right. I wonder about the savvy."

"What do you mean . . . the savvy?"

"The wisdom. The God-given brains to make a real cow-man."

Stormy lifted the saddle, hung it from a peg by one stirrup, and gazed at it. The seating leather shone dully; the scratches were mellowed, faded. Colville scratches. He turned and thumbed back his hat. Buttrick was watching him. "I was raised with cattle, Colonel," he said.

Buttrick nodded. "I didn't mean that. I've already heard you're as good a roper and all-around hand as we've ever had in the valley. It's other things. You'll understand what I mean when the time comes. It all looks pretty easy from where you stand now. Too easy, maybe. Well . . . time'll tell." The colonel walked with his springy stride out of the barn and Stormy's flickering little smile followed him.

The ranch fell into a kind of languor as the hot hours went by. From the bunkhouse came the drone of voices and short outbursts of profanity. There was a poker game in progress. Once the howl of Deefy Hunt rose, shrill and crackling, and Holk Peters's exuberant laugh followed it.

Stormy took down his saddle, lugged it around to the corral, caught his black horse, rigged up, and rode northwest, keeping the barn between himself and the house.

A coyote, worrying a rabbit's defunct carcass, threw up its head when the long man's shadow swept near. The animal's nearly human eyes, light and tawny with a million years of craft in them, watched. The coyote's tongue came out. He panted.

Four blackish streaks rose from a tangle of plum thicket near the meandering creek that supplied the home ranch, heaped shrill imprecations on horse and rider because they had frightened them, flew in indignant circles, then came back to rest in the thicket again. Stormy watched them a moment, reined off his course toward the thicket, and found what he expected, a new-born calf, dark red, slimy sleek, lying in a puddle, the cow standing above her offspring, red-eyed and anxious, watching the magpies, knowing in her dark instincts they would pick out the calf's eyes if she relaxed her vigilance a moment. At sight of the rider, she dropped her head still lower, facing this new threat.

Stormy stopped, rubbed his palm over the cool butt of his holstered belt gun, longed to blast the feathered marauders, but didn't because the echo would carry back to the ranch. He dismounted, threw stones. His aim was inaccurate, but the big birds fled notwithstanding, screeching, whirling higher and higher before they decided the man thing wasn't going to leave, then they flew eastward.

Stormy re-mounted, cast a long look at the cow, turned, and rode on, but slowly, and now he stayed along the creek where there was a scent of coolness and rotting leaves, and cattle. Stayed with the creek until he came to a lift in the land, up which he rode and stopped on the shimmering crest, looking backward. Nowhere down the long slope of valley was there sign of another rider. He shrugged, rode across the land with waves of heat for companions until he saw the darker green of heavy growth, the sturdy upthrusts of trees against the still, pale sky. Cap-Rock Spring.

In the shade again the black horse cropped grass, dragging his reins, careful not to step on them and bruise his mouth. Once he went over beside the man, nuzzled the water, set up widening arcs of ripple, sipped a little, and drifted away.

Stormy made a cigarette, his hat on the grass beside him, his eyes pinpointed on the brown paper trough, the flakes of tinder-dry tobacco. When he lit the match, its flare was feeble, making no impression on the orange hue of daylight. He snapped it, dropped it, and watched the concentric circles widen in the spring.

If she came, which he began to doubt now, it would be the same as it had been that first time, as it had been last night. His gaze hardened. Smoke riffled upward past his nose, his forehead. No, it didn't have to be the same. Irritably he looked away from the pool. Almost bitterly his mind told him it didn't *have* to be the same always, but it would be; they were so much alike.

"Dammit," he said aloud, squirming into a more comfortable position on the ground. Then he thought of Walter Proctor, their talk, and a cold hardness came into his eyes. One thing was certain; he'd run MVP from now on and it would be a different ranch. First off there'd be the new foreman. He thought then of Slim and Slim's withdrawal around him since he and Jerry and Holystone had returned from Fort Burnett. With a start something hit his consciousness. Slim Thatcher was in love with Jerry!

He held perfectly still, adjusting to the obvious, which he'd failed to see before. Slim Thatcher—gray hair, squinty look, leather-colored hide, long, angular frame, ten years too old. He wondered how such a thing had come to be. What could Slim have hoped for; he was as plain, as colorless, as Jerry was handsome. Contempt grew. Stormy drew pleasure from the prospect of Slim's silent agony.

It simplified something, though. Thatcher's love for Jerry; now Slim would ride on. No, not Slim. He'd hang around MVP as a rider. He was the dog-loyal type.

Stormy thought back to Slim's innuendo about him and Toni last night. He squirmed; his fingers pressed the narrow body of the cigarette. That had been a tomfool thing to do. If he'd thought—but he hadn't, and she'd taunted him to it. His anger turned upon Toni Buttrick. Being like she was, she'd probably engineered it like that on purpose, had known they'd be missed. Did it as much to taunt Jerry as prove she could make Stormy obey. He'd have to watch that green-eyed witch; there was enough treachery in her to make a fool out of a calculating man and love doing it.

He lay back, watching the soft-shadowed leaves overhead lie with flat darkness against the sky. She was cruel, too, each kiss told him that. His glance hardened. He understood that kind, man or woman. From now on if anyone were endangered, dared, it wouldn't be him.

A hot little breeze played high in the trees, swooped lower, tumbled among the brush and grass, then lifted itself with a bored and searching exuberance and ran away with a soft moaning.

# CHAPTER ELEVEN

He waited two hours and was standing up, dusting leaf mold off his legs when he heard the creak of saddle leather, the jingle of rein chains. He looked up and around and saw her. He remained standing in that twisted way until she came up and dismounted, walking around to the head of her horse. He straightened up. She let the reins slip through her fingers. Her horse moved away, deeper into the shade where the black horse was. It was an MVP animal, one he recognized as a favorite of Slim Thatcher's.

"Well?"

He smiled at her. "I thought you said you weren't coming."

She sank down on the grass near the spring. It was cool and shadowy there with the brush and trees around. She shrugged. "You didn't bring me . . . curiosity did. What do you want to talk about?"

He sank down again. She wore a plain white blouse that fitted her well. It lay open at the throat and threw the outline of her bosom boldly forward. Her long mouth was solemn, almost sullen. The taunting arrogance wasn't there and her green eyes were pensive. She had her long legs drawn up, arms folded around them, bending forward a little to look into the water. "We could talk about a lot of things," he said.

She threw him a sharp look. "It was a ruse, wasn't it, getting me out here? You didn't want to talk."

"Yes, I did," he said, leaning back and looking up at her. "But

I don't know how to say it."

The green eyes studied his face. "I can't help you," she said.

He reached over and took her arm, pulled her back beside him. She went without a struggle, but her eyes smoldered at him. Lying back, gazing up, she said: "Can you talk better this way?" There was bitterness in her face.

He smiled at her, bent low, and kissed her lightly, moving his mouth on hers. Then he pulled back a little. "You did that last night on purpose. To see if I'd be down there at the corral. All right, maybe I did this the same way . . . for the same reason."

She rolled her head sideways, not looking at him. The bitterness was in her voice. "I thought that was it," she said. "I came. Now we're even."

"Good," he said quickly. "I'll take your dares and you'll take mine. That's settled and past, then. We know each other that well now."

"And . . . from here . . . where do we go?" She still avoided his gaze.

He put one thick arm across her. "Wherever you want to go."

"That's impossible," she said. "You're married."

"I was just as married last night."

Her lips parted, hung slackly. "Why did you do it, Stormy? Why? You knew there was something between us that night at Big B. Why did you marry *her?*"

"I didn't know anything about you that night at Big B, except that you had green eyes . . . were willing . . . that night."

"Well, dammit," she said. "Wasn't that enough to know?"

"It still is."

She struggled up under his weight, turned her face to avoid his lips, and felt rigid to him. He slacked off, moved up just enough to sit beside her. Behind them the horses made faint, soft sounds as they moved.

"What can we have this way, Stormy?"

"Each other," he said.

She turned on him with a fierceness. "If you think. . . ."

He stifled the wrath with a kiss, forcing her down again, holding her pinioned with his shoulders. Pressing his mouth against hers, she responded with a furious encircling of his neck, a tightening of her long mouth over his, and a savage flooding of emotion. It was different from Jerry's way of making love. It was primitive and raging. He responded with cruel retaliation, with brutal tenderness, the kind that Toni Buttrick was made for. She didn't fight him, but her urge to hurt him as he hurt her made her twist and gouge his flesh with her fingers. Then he let her go and she didn't move. Instead of hot, stinging tears that Jerry had shown, Toni's green gaze was still and dry, darker by shades than it had been before, dark, emerald green.

"All right," she said finally. "I've always told myself, if I ever found the man I wanted, I'd take him if I had to kill to get him. I'd take him any way I could get him. That ought to make your pride feel good, Stormy."

He lay back on the grass beside her. A long, silent exhalation of breath escaped him and inside was triumph. He talked and she listened, now and then interrupting waspishly, almost defiantly, but what she said wasn't always coherent or sensible. Mostly she just listened, keeping her green gaze on the ragged old clouds that ran tirelessly southward overhead, seen through treetops.

"He loves you, doesn't he?"

"Who?"

He twisted his head to look at her. "You aren't listening."

"Yes, I am. I'm listening."

"I said Carus Smith's in love with you."

"Yes, he is. What about it?"

"Well . . . ?"

"I couldn't care less, Stormy. Carus is a brother, not a lover."

"He'd make you a good husband."

She made a hard chuckle. "It looks like I don't want a husband, doesn't it? At least I'm apparently not supposed to have one. A lover, Stormy, not a husband . . . I think that's what I want. No . . . I don't *want* it like that, but it's to be that way, I suppose."

They talked for an hour more. He dwelt on Carus Smith quite a bit because an idea had taken shape in his mind. It had crystallized gradually as they'd lain there, and finally, when he got up and went over to bring back the horses, he knew what course he'd follow with her.

It pleased him that he'd humbled her arrogance, ground down her pride, her vaguely shown superiority. What meant the most, however, was the certainty that through her he'd get the other half of the valley—and Carus Smith would help him to do it without knowing it at all.

He helped her to mount and nodded at the horse. "That's Slim Thatcher's pet rope horse."

"I know," she said. "I used that as my excuse for going riding. I told Dad and Slim I'd like to try him, maybe trade for him." The green eyes grew sardonically amused. "You should've seen Dad's expression."

"What about Slim?"

She looked down at him for a moment without speaking. "He didn't say much. You know, Stormy, he's got something else on his mind. He loves Jerry . . . you know that, don't you?"

He shrugged. "I reckon so."

Her irony deepened, went into her voice. "You've made a first-class enemy out of Slim Thatcher. Don't underestimate him, Stormy, he's rawhide and wily."

His boldness came up to show carelessly. "I won't underestimate him, Toni. I've got him pegged for what he is."

She leaned a little from the saddle. "I don't think you know

Slim very well, Stormy. He was quite a man before I went away to school."

That time he smiled. "I was, too," he said.

She snugged up the reins, lifted them, was going to say something when he put his hand on her horse's neck and moved up beside her. "Toni, one week from today I'll be on that ridge that runs east-west above Big B. Meet me there."

She rode away without agreeing or demurring, and he stood back in the long shadows watching her slimness, then he cast a long look at the sun, read the time, and mounted his own animal. He rode due north until he was on the upthrusts above Marais Valley, then he cut south, and poked along, giving her plenty of time to get back first.

# CHAPTER TWELVE

Evening found Stormy Merrill behind the ranch buildings. He'd made a southerly swoop that brought him into the yard from behind the Proctor house. The first man he met was Holk Peters, emerging from the kitchen via the rear door. Holk was making a cigarette. He glanced up and smiled at Stormy.

"What'd you do, fall asleep under a tree somewhere?"

Stormy swung down and walked beside Holk toward the barn. "That's exactly what I did," he said, walking as slowly, as casually as Holk was walking, but looking around the yard from beneath his hat brim. There was a guttering glow of light from the bunkhouse. Holk nodded his head at it. "I ain't too popular in there right now. Won eleven dollars offen Deefy Hunt. The others are still playing. Bob Thorne was ahead when I come over to eat."

"Big B staying over another night?" Stormy asked.

"Yeah. The colonel and Mister Proctor said this only happens once a lifetime and it's good for the outfits."

Holk followed Stormy into the barn, smoked idly, and watched the black horse get divested of his rigging, be turned into a big box stall, and fed. He hunkered in the doorway, and leaned back against the siding as Stormy came out, stood close by twisting up a cigarette of his own.

"Golly, I feel good," Holk said for no particular reason.

Stormy lit up and squatted. "I reckon you do. How much've you won lately, altogether?"

"Sixty-seven dollars." Holk squirmed against the log wall. "I got enough to buy a new saddle up at Burnett . . . only I never get a chance t'go up there."

"Won't Slim let you off?"

"Naw. I wanted t'go up when you and Holystone went, but he said no."

Stormy smoked thoughtfully for several minutes, until his cigarette was burned down. When he stood up, he hitched at his sagging shell belt and pistol, said he'd see Holk later, and went around the side of the main house to the kitchen door, entered, and nodded at Cookie, who was sitting sprawled at the big table, drinking coffee.

The muddy old eyes watched Stormy cross to the table and sink down. Cookie flagged with a pulpy hand toward the coffee pot on a back burner of the stove. "Draw a cup," he said, and Stormy was surprised at the geniality in the old man's voice. He filled a cup, went back, and sat down again.

"You're hungry," Cookie said matter-of-factly. "Only time I get visitors is when they're hungry." Cookie made no move to rise. He sipped his coffee. "Sure some wingding last night, warn't it?"

"Yeah, everybody seemed to have had a good time."

Cookie laughed softly. "If the house's any sign, why, I expect they had the times of their lives. Place looks like a herd o' bulls been run through it." He grunted pleasantly. "Good thing for folks to let down once in a while." He looked across the table at Stormy. "You married into a good outfit, if you don't mind my saying so."

Stormy said nothing; his glance was distantly cool and fully on the cook's face.

Cookie reddened, struggled to his feet, and said: "Want some cold T-bone?"

"That sounds good, yeah."

Cookie fumbled in the floor-to-ceiling cooler, brought out a platter of withered, cold meat, selected a piece, tossed it onto a plate with some beans, scooped up a knife and fork, and put them all carelessly before Stormy. "Y'know," he said, unaffected by the snub, "someday beef's going to be worth real money again, and when it is, places like MVP and Big B are going to be rich." The rheumy eyes curved down to Stormy's face, averted, bent low over the food. "If a young feller like you's able to make things hum, you'll wind up with everything you want."

Stormy bobbed his head while his jaws worked, his mind on Toni Buttrick. When he'd finished eating, he put up his dish and implements, went back outside, stood on the gallery, and smelled the night, heard the house coming to life around in front, the guffaws of men, the husky laughter of his wife. To his right a long dagger of lamplight laid athwart the gallery floor from under the door of Walter Proctor's office, He considered it for a time, then turned toward it. He knocked, and Proctor called out for him to enter.

Inside, the big man dwarfed his roll-top desk. Several battered chairs were strewn around the room. Some cigar butts lay near a green cuspidor. On the walls were Indian trophies, branding irons that were burned out, no longer usable. A crudely made wooden box on a spindly table next to the desk held a bulging, slovenly collection of dust-laden papers, records.

"Sit down, Stormy. Glad you came around." Walter dipped a big hand, came up holding a bottle of whiskey. "Have a drink."

Stormy drank. The stuff burned unmercifully, almost gagged him. Walter Proctor took a long drink and showed nothing but a slightly heightened reddening of the face and Stormy's first suspicion was confirmed. Proctor was an alcoholic of long standing; perhaps he had a bad heart, too, but foremost he was a drinker. Maybe Jerry didn't know; more likely she knew and refused to name her father's ailment correctly. At any rate her father's heavy reliance on Slim Thatcher, the condition of the ranch yard, Proctor's slip-shod methods, his slovenliness, all stemmed directly from addiction to alcohol in excessive amounts. Stormy shoved his legs out from the chair, let his eyebrows go low. Slim Thatcher. . . .

"What's on your mind, Stormy? Want to know how to run a big ranch?"

"In time, I reckon," Stormy said. "But first off I'd like to know what you'd think of suggestions for a few changes."

Walter looked blank. There were mottled blue veins under his eyes, a more-than-ever marked pallor to his face. "Changes? What kind of changes?"

"Big ones, Walter." Stormy watched the flushed face, the watery eyes.

"Well, now, Stormy," Walter said uneasily. "MVP's been around a long time. It's made money. Not much since the war, maybe, but a living for all of us. Now then . . . changes. . . ." Walter wagged his head warily. "What kind of changes?"

Stormy was feeling his way, picking over words for the right ones. "For one thing, Walt, the place needs a cleaning up. It's run down. Junk's been thrown everywhere. Big B's clean as a hound's tooth next to MVP. For another thing . . . too many big bull calves on the range. We didn't get them all by a damned sight on the roundup. I know. I saw a lot we never caught at all."

"Well, but, Stormy, we can't get them *all*, you know that. Our tallies show us with a big increase. . . ."

"I know," Stormy said, "but what we miss on roundup'd make the increase bigger. That'd mean more profit, bigger herds to drive to rail's end for sale. Anyway, Walter, those calves aren't all good for breeding-stock. Spindly butted, long-legged, more longhorn than shorthorn. Best price's fetched on beefy types. That means we've got to have good bulls, not cull bulls."

"Yes," Walter said slowly, thickly, looking at the bottle, near his elbow on the desk. "That's the way folks're getting to think, only Stormy . . . it's the numbers you sell that make money."

Stormy shook his head. "That used to be the way. Nowadays when you trail a herd of tent poles to rail's end you know damned well the buyers'll take the best herds first. That means scrub stuff brings lowest price. The best sold aren't tent-pole critters."

Walter leaned back, his chair protesting gratingly. He curled a huge fist around the bottle, pulled it closer, but didn't lift it. Stormy watched him, clear-eyed, mind like a poised dagger, saw the profiled chins, the pastiness of the flesh, and the bluish run of mottled color in Walter's cheeks, his nose, the ill look to his mouth and eyes. Heard the heavy, uneven breathing. He leaned forward and held out his hand.

"I'd like another drink, Walt."

Walter handed him the bottle, watched his Adam's apple bobble, took the bottle almost gratefully, and drank from it himself with longer swallows, shorter pauses. He pushed the bottle back from him and gazed steadily at Stormy while the coursing fire spread out fanwise in his belly. He smiled. "I guess," he said slackly. "I guess. . . ."

Stormy watched the watery gaze blur. He couldn't read sense into what Walter had started to say or in his expression, either.

"What?"

Proctor fought to gather his wandering wits. "Well," he said thickly, "all right. We can send the wagon out again. Comb the uplands and the valley again. Get the strays and hide-outs and cut them."

Stormy leaned forward. "Would you do it my way, this time?"

Walter's slackness vanished a little. His eyes grew harassed, wary. "How's that?" he said. "You in charge of the wagon?"

"No. Sam in charge of the wagon. Sam in charge, Holk Peters and Holystone and Cookie with him."

"What about Slim?"

"Slim here on the ranch . . . cleaning up the place."

Walter looked startled, shocked. "Oh," he said finally, pain-fully, "you couldn't do *that*. Leave Holystone or Holk to clean up. You couldn't put Slim to choring like that."

Stormy grew intent. "Walter," he said, "Slim's a top hand, but it wouldn't have been necessary to send the wagon back out if he hadn't missed so damned many hide-outs. I've got nothing especially against Slim, but MVP's got to get hold of its bootstraps and lift, if it's going to get ahead. Slim's too easy. He isn't the man for foreman."

The room sweltered in silence. It was so deep, so acoustically sharp that other sounds came readily into the office, sounds of laughter and music from around in front, in the partying sec-tion of the old house. Walter ran a fleshy hand over his face and looked at the mass of papers on his desk. His fingers shook. He swiveled around more in the chair and swatted aimlessly at a fly that lit on one heavy thigh. "I was afraid something like this might happen," he said, troubled.

Stormy was still sitting forward in his chair. "You want MVP run right, don't you? You don't want things to keep falling apart, getting worse like they're going to get if something isn't done to stop them." Stormy's voice changed, became vibrant, knife-edged. He was playing his trump. "Listen, Walt, MVP's going downhill. Damned if I'm going to pull my guts out on a ranch that's backsliding. I'd rather go west and get an outfit of my own." He stopped there, let the silence seep in and saturate the atmosphere. And he watched Walter Proctor's face.

It took a long time—a lot of conflict—but finally Jerry's father pushed crooked fingers that shook through his mop of hair and looked glassily at his son-in-law. "Shouldn't we go slow on these changes?" he asked plaintively. "Slim's been around MVP a long time, Stormy."

Stormy thought: *Too long.* He said: "It isn't Slim. It's the way things are going here. Maybe if I took her west we could. . . ."

"All right," Walter said leadenly. "All right . . . only. . . ."

Stormy stood up with triumph inside him and behind the mask of his face. "Don't worry about Slim, Walt. He'll understand. He's got a lot of savvy."

Walter looked up swiftly. "But don't you tell him," he said. "Let me do that."

# CHAPTER THIRTEEN

Stormy left Walt in the soft, mellow light of the office. He walked with a bold stride around the gallery to the front of the house where lamplight fell with golden yellow beauty, and there he caught sight of Jerry. She saw him and hurried out of the house, swept up close, and looked into his face. Almost breathlessly she said: "Where have you been all day, darling?"

He told her, instead, of his talk with her father, its import and meaning, and, as he knew it would do, it made her totally unmindful of the lost hours he didn't account for.

"Oh . . . not Slim," she said. "Stormy, he'll quit. He'll ride away. He's been foreman so long." Her words trailed off as a long, lean shadow emerged from the doorway and a soft-drawling voice said: "Did I hear someone blessing me out?"

Stormy looked past Jerry and saw the gray hair curling upward from Slim's ears, the perpetually squinted eyes. Very gently he touched his wife. "Go on inside, Jerry. Keep your party going." He turned toward the taller, thinner man. "Take a walk with me, Slim."

They moved away from the house, side-by-side. Slim shot one inquiring glance, then didn't look at Stormy again. They went past the barn where night shade made a pool of square blackness deeper than any shadow, and, when Stormy came to the corral, he hung one booted foot over a pole and leaned a shoulder against the upper poles, looking squarely at the foreman.

"It wasn't supposed to work out this way, Slim," he said in his too-gentle voice. "Walt was supposed to tell you, but you heard part of what my wife and I were talking about, I expect, so I'll give you the rest of it."

Thatcher stood, wide-legged, and made no attempt to keep the coldness, the antagonism out of his face. "Let me guess," he said. "I'm fired."

"No, not fired, Slim, but Sam Oberlin's going to be foreman."

The bronzed face split in a death's-head grin, bitter and bleak. "Sam? Why, I figured you'd be taking that job. Seems I under-guessed you, Merrill. Foreman wouldn't be good enough for you, would it? You're a pardner. Pardners don't ramrod outfits, do they?"

The taunting bluntness, the strong dislike, undiluted, went into Stormy and aroused the cruel streak. He, too, smiled, calculating to hit Thatcher where it would hurt him most, and knowing how to do it. His smile was as lacking in humor as Thatcher's was, but he had triumph where Thatcher had none. "Go ahead," he said. "Get it out of your system."

But Slim stopped speaking, put one arm over the top pole of the corral, and leaned there. After a while he said: "Naw, I've got nothing to say, really. I reckon I saw this coming. You married a ranch and you've got all the rights. I got none." The puckered eyes were unblinkingly on Stormy's face. "All right, feller, you won hands down. She's yours, her and the outfit. I got a choice. I can ride on or step down to forty a month. Well, Merrill, I'm going to tell you this much . . . I'll stay. I'll take Sam's orders and be an MVP rider. Do you want to know why?"

"Sure, why?"

"Because I don't think you'll be around very long."

Slim was moving away, his back to Stormy, when the thick fist shot out, caught his arm, and whirled him back again. The too-gentle voice said: "What makes you think that, Slim?"

But the answer to that had to wait. Slim shook free of the arm Stormy had grabbed with a blazing wild light in his eyes. "Listen, Stormy," he said thickly, "don't ever lay a hand on me again. Never."

Stormy ignored the fury. "Why did you say that?" The boldness, the antagonism, was up in the younger man's face. His mouth was a slit that bore the harshness of a cruel, downward pull.

"Why? Because I don't think you'll last, that's all." The fire faded from Thatcher's face. "You're not the staying kind. You or Sam Oberlin. You ride in, hang and rattle a while, then blow out again. I don't know where you came from . . . you or Sam . . . and I don't give a damn, but neither of you is the staying kind."

Wishing to hurt and knowing how to do it, Stormy said: "Well . . . if you're right and I drift on, Slim, I'll take the one thing from MVP that'll be like taking the guts and heart out of it. You can figure that out for yourself."

They stood nearly toe to toe in silence. Where antagonism had been before, hatred grew and matured. Slim Thatcher said: "I know what you mean. That don't need much figuring." Then he turned and walked out across the yard, and the moonlight made him taller, thinner than he was.

Stormy's cold gaze stayed with the retreating figure. He gripped a corral pole with one hand, wondering what Slim Thatcher would tell Walter Proctor. He didn't care. Anyway Slim was gentle. He wouldn't say anything to Walter or Jerry to deepen the anguish that was creeping like a blight over MVP.

When he finally went back to the house, Jerry caught him, drew him out onto the floor, and danced with him, searching his face, keeping instinctive time to the fiddle, guitar, and mouth-organ music.

"What happened, Stormy? Slim came in looking like a ghost."

"I told him he wasn't foreman any more."

"But . . . not like that."

Stormy held her close, feeling the movement of her against him. "I wanted to make it easy, Jerry. He got hot. I didn't blame him. It's pretty hard for a man to step down like that. Well . . . it didn't amount to much anyway. A few words."

She dropped her head to his shoulder, let it rest there, but her gun-metal eyes were large and shadowed with unhappiness. When the dance was over, she led him to the sideboard.

"Would you like me to fix you a plate?"

"No," she said, "I'm not hungry. Stormy . . . what did he say?"

"Slim? Not a hell of a lot. I thought he'd quit, ride on, but he's going to stay." He shook his head. "I wouldn't have."

"He's been here so long," she said, watching Sam Oberlin spearing food nearby, dark face averted, eyes roaming over the food as though it was his only consideration on earth. "Does Dad know?"

"I don't think so . . . not yet," Stormy said, turning toward her and out of the corner of his eye seeing Toni Buttrick watching them from across the room. "He was supposed to tell Slim, not me, but, when Slim heard us on the porch, I figured I might as well do it."

"It would have been better if Dad had done it."

He flushed, turned on her fiercely. "You act like he was kinfolk, Jerry."

"He almost is," she said, seeing the anger in his face.

"Well, from now on he's just another rider. Like Holystone or Holk."

"Are you going to ramrod things, Stormy?"

"No, Sam is."

"Oh."

He moved around her, past her, toward Sam, whose dark

eyes smiled at him. Together they strolled over to a corner and faced toward the room, watching the others. Moodily Stormy said: "You're foreman starting from right now, Sam."

"Yeah? Does Slim know it?"

"He knows it. We just talked about it outside."

The dark eyes slewed around the room, found Slim, and stayed on him. "He don't look very pleased," Sam said around a mouthful of food.

Stormy looked at Thatcher without seeming to. "I wouldn't be, either," he said.

Slim was accosted by Colonel Buttrick. In the background Toni moved. Carus Smith and Bob Thorne were talking to her and among themselves. Something stirred in Stormy's mind. He looked around at Sam. "Where's that spider-legged Big B rider and Holystone?"

"Hunt? Him and Holystone got to Holystone's lumbago liniment. They're both sleeping it off in the bunkhouse. Got as loop-legged as two damned fools can get. Old Buttrick came within an ace of firing Deefy. I believe he would have, too, if Deefy could've heard what Buttrick was saying to him."

Sam stopped speaking. His head swiveled slowly, watching Slim Thatcher cross the room to the doorway, and go outside onto the gallery. Sam looked more amused than curious and spoke aside to Stormy. "Slim's going to hunt up Proctor and cry in his lap."

Stormy grunted, shrugged. "Naw, he's too loyal to Proctor to say very much. But I don't care if he does. Proctor and I had it all talked out before I told Slim."

"Well," Sam said, laying aside the empty dish. "What you got in mind now . . . boss?"

"First off, Sam, you'll take Cookie, Holystone, and Holk, and go back out with the wagon, catch every hide-out bull calf you can find, cut every blessed one of them, and make a new tally."

He looked around at Oberlin. "You've got to make a good showing, Sam. I told old Proctor Slim'd missed a lot of stuff. You understand?"

"I think so," Sam said slowly. "You want a bigger tally, so's Proctor'll really believe Slim didn't work the range like he should've. That right?"

"Yeah."

Sam's dark eyes glowed. "That'll be easy," he said.

"Get them all," Stormy said. "Make the new tally good enough to show Slim up. Take plenty of time and scour the range."

Sam smiled dourly. "I've been around a few years," he said. "I'll make a good showing. I'll make it so good Proctor'll think you're real modest."

"That's what I want. I want Proctor to eat out of my hand and this'll be half the battle."

"And what about Slim?"

Stormy's glance grew hot and shiny. "Slim's going to stay behind and clean up the yard, get the barn dunged out, and generally make the place around here look like Big B looks."

Sam pursed his lips into a silent whistle. "He isn't going to like that. Who tells him, you or me?"

"You do. You're foreman. If you don't want to, I will. And I don't give a damn whether he likes it or don't like it." The musicians were back on their chairs against the wall. "What I'd like," Stormy continued, "would be for him to slope. The more I think of it, the less I like the idea of him hanging around here." The music started and Colonel Buttrick made a beeline for Jerry. Carus Smith swung Toni. Stormy watched the dancers without interest. "Sam, does Slim know anything about you? Has he ever asked any questions about you . . . or me?"

"No, of course not. Why?"

"I just wondered. He made the remark down by the corrals

that neither you nor me is the kind that stay around a place very long."

Sam's face grew thoughtful. Gradually it cleared. "He must've meant we're restless. He's never asked me about you and he don't know a damned thing about me."

"All right."

But Sam was still exploring the notion. "It'll pay to keep an eye on him, maybe," he said. "Maybe it's good he isn't going to ride on, Stormy."

"Maybe. I guess you're right."

"Then don't get him sore enough to quit. He's just the kind that could snort up trouble for both of us."

"He won't quit . . . not Thatcher. He'll be around when the last dog's hung."

The dance ended. Colonel Buttrick led Jerry back to her chair and leaned a little from the waist to talk to her. Stormy saw Slim come back into the room. He was moving sluggishly, eyes blank and dull-looking. Holystone made a stumbling entrance, teetered in the bright light, blinking moistly. Stormy crossed the room to him. The scent of liquor was strong ten feet away. He took the old rider's arm, turned him, and propelled him back outside. A taller, younger shadow was leaning against the gallery upright across from the door, trying to make a cigarette with fingers that lacked even a semblance of coordination. Stormy pulled Holystone down where the rosebush was and pressed down on his shoulders. Holystone sank onto a little wooden bench.

"Holystone, can you hear me?"

The brimming eyes lifted vacantly, an annoyed frown looked imbecilic. "Hear you?" Holystone said. " 'Course I can hear you. What'd you think, I'm blind?"

"Go on back to the bunkhouse . . . you and Hunt . . . and stay there."

"Say," Holystone said with solemn indignation, squaring scrawny shoulders. "Who the hell you giving orders to, anyway. It's Stormy, ain't it?"

"Yeah, it's Stormy. Now do like I said. Go on down there and finish sleeping it off."

Holystone groped for the edge of the bench, gripped it with a talon-like fist, and started to rise. Stormy put a detaining hand on his shoulder and held him down. Holystone squirmed.

"Take you cussed claw offen me, Stormy, damn you. Who'n hell you think you are . . . giving orders . . . anyway."

"Who?" Stormy said, bending low. "I'm the feller who just made Sam Oberlin foreman and Slim Thatcher a common rider. That's who I am, and if you don't like what I say, you can draw your time and drift. Understand?"

Holystone's vague gaze grew still. His mouth dropped open, hung slackly in an effort to comprehend something. The pink shininess of his tongue shone in the moonlight. He rallied after a moment and spoke. "You couldn't do that, Stormy. You couldn't put Sam in Slim's place. Mist' Proctor . . . only he could do that."

"Mister Proctor could do it . . . but I've already done it. Mister Proctor and I talked it over before I did it." Stormy's fist on Holystone's shoulder closed around the shirt, the scraggly old flesh underneath, and brought Holystone to his feet. "Now go on back there to the bunkhouse, Holystone, and stay there." He gave the old rider a little shove. Holystone's warped legs, never too steady, sagged. Deefy Hunt, cigarette spilled and forgotten, caught Holystone as he lurched, held him up with one hand, and fixed a belligerent stare on Stormy.

"No call for rough stuff," he said. There was a willingness to fight in his pale eyes.

Stormy's lip curled. "You'd better see him to bed, Big B," he said. "I don't want either of you hanging around the house in the shape you're in. Go on."

He watched Hunt turn with his burden, start for the bunkhouse in a meandering way, and he heard Holystone's voice raised in garrulous indignation over the demotion of Slim Thatcher. It pleased Stormy to hear it.

Toni Buttrick's sarcasm came out of the doorway to him. "What's the matter, MVP, afraid they'll contaminate the ladies . . . or just want to see how it feels to spread your new wings a little?"

He went over to her. The old green taunt was up in her eyes, the long mouth was parted, inviting, daring. "What new wings are you talking about?"

"Don't act so naïve, Texas," she said. "Everybody knows you've taken over MVP, demoted Slim Thatcher, put that Oberlin half-breed in his place."

He blinked at her. "Who knows, and who told you?"

"Honey," she said, watching the way the shadows worked flat angles across his face, "the colonel told me. I think he got it from Walter Proctor . . . before Proctor passed out. He's around in his office, Dad told me, drunker than a lord, sprawled out on his desk and dead to the world. But everyone knows, anyway. Can't you see how the party's cooling. Look at the way the men are acting. Slim is a pretty popular man in Marais Valley, Texas. I hope you didn't stub your toe this time. Anyway . . . it's like an epidemic has settled over the house . . . over MVP."

He gazed at her in silence for a moment, then brushed past her into the room and said over his shoulder: "One week from today on that hill above your place."

Jerry didn't smile at him as he sat down beside her. Holk Peters was loitering nearby, struggling with his courage. After Stormy had come up, Holk's half-won battle to ask Jerry to dance dissolved like smoke. He drifted aimlessly toward the food-laden sideboard.

"What's the matter, Jerry?"

"Dad," she said. "I went around to the office to see why he wasn't in here. It didn't look right, his not coming in for just a little while, anyway."

"And?"

"He's . . . drunk. He's lying across his desk drunk."

Stormy looked across the room when a burst of laughter erupted. Carus Smith had Holk by the arm, was presenting him to Toni. Holk was squirming, beet-red and tongue-tied. Stormy looked down at his wife again, saw the dark profusion of eyelashes, low over the gray-black eyes, the closed mouth, heavy and soft-looking.

"Do you want me to go around and see if I can buck him up?"

"Well . . . you can't sober him up, I know, but could you and . . . could you and one of the boys put him to bed?"

"Sure." He reached over, touched her hands where they lay closed in her lap. "This is what you meant when you said he had heart trouble, isn't it?"

She moved her fingers. "Not exactly. He does have heart trouble, but I suppose I meant this more than the heart trouble . . . really."

He stood up. "All right. You keep the party going. Sam and I'll put him to bed."

Sam was on the gallery, smoking. Stormy brushed past him and breathed a word: "C'mon."

They entered the office and were immediately struck by the smell, as strong as lye, of whiskey. Sam pursed his mouth in the dry-whistling way he had and his black eyes swung to the massive hulk of Walter Proctor. "He's got a skin full, Stormy."

Stormy showed more disgust than anything else. He took Proctor by the shaggy mane and pulled him off the desk. The big body slumped, the chair groaned, and Sam ran a glance over Proctor's inert shape.

"We might lift him, Stormy, but we aren't going to pack him very far."

They got him onto their arms by Indian-locking fists beneath his gross weight. It was when they straightened, bringing the hulk out of the chair so that their shoulders quivered with strain and their breath came short and choppy. Stormy grated a curse, began to move in a mincing, knee-sprung way. They made slow progress toward the opened door in the room's north wall beyond which was a partially seen bureau and bedstead.

Sam said: "Is this where he sleeps?"

Stormy grunted again, louder. "I don't know and don't care. This is where we're going to dump him."

They got the inert, soggy weight through the door and to the bed, dumped it there, and both were seized with a strange lightness, as though they would leave the ground. Sam groped for an end of the bed and hung on. He was watching Stormy and breathing deeply.

Behind them at the door there was a sound. Both men turned. Colonel Buttrick was standing, framed in the opening, lean, thin face gazing past them at the disarrayed pile of Walter Proctor sprawled on the bed. No one spoke.

The colonel came into the room slowly. He raised his glance to Stormy. There was something hard and solid in his gaze. "You don't understand this, I suppose," he said. "It's a little different from getting hog drunk in a saloon or sporting house. Getting petrified at your own daughter's wedding celebration." The bloodless mouth widened into a chilly grin. "I hope you never have to understand this, Merrill. I reckon I ought to hope something else for you, too . . . that you never have a daughter."

Stormy looked across the colonel's bent back at Sam. He made a slow, sardonic wink. "It's all right with me, Colonel," he said callously. "I've bundled a lot of drunks into their bunks in my time."

Buttrick came up slowly and stiffly. His eyes were frostily unpleasant. "I suppose you have," he said acidly. "Only this happens to be a different kind of a drunk, Merrill." The flinty gaze remained fixed on Stormy's face.

Stormy felt the long, steady, penetrating stare and his anger stirred under its coldness. In a silky way he said: "Put it into plain words, Colonel."

But Colonel Buttrick was bending over the bed once more, unmindful and unanswering.

Adrift in the room's hush and unpleasantness, Stormy jerked his head at Sam. They went back out into the office and Sam offered his tobacco sack. Stormy went to work twisting up a cigarette with a solid feeling of antagonism rising within him toward Colonel Buttrick. Sam made a smoke, too, got it going off Stormy's match, and said through the smoke in a quiet voice: "I think you said the wrong thing to old hatchet-face. He don't like you, either. That makes two, tonight . . . Slim and Buttrick."

Stormy looked into the black eyes. "You can carve another notch pretty quick now, Sam. Add Carus Smith. He doesn't know it yet, but he's going to hate my guts worse'n poison one of these days."

Sam said nothing, but wore a speculative expression and looked at the mass of papers scattered over the desk and on the floor of the room.

Stormy used his finger to knock ashes off his quirly and was moving toward the door when Colonel Buttrick appeared in the bedroom doorway with a white ridge in the flesh above his upper lip.

"Merrill."

Stormy turned. A sharp electric shock passed between the two men.

Buttrick rolled his head backward. "Come in here a moment."

Stormy went. Sam stood where he was, watching, letting smoke tumble gently from his parted lips.

Stormy entered the bedroom and looked at the older man. Buttrick motioned toward the bed with one hand. "Go take a look at him," he said.

Stormy went over by the bed. Buttrick had moved Walter Proctor so that he lay straight and relaxed on the bed, arms at his sides, collar open, face composed, eyes half open.

It struck Stormy like a hammer blow. He straightened up and half turned to face the colonel. "He's dead," he said.

Colonel Buttrick inclined his head. "Yes, he is, isn't he? Quite dead. Too little heart, too much liquor." Then he left the room and Sam appeared in the doorway, staring first at Walter Proctor, then at Stormy inquiringly.

# CHAPTER FOURTEEN

Holk Peters and Holystone of MVP, and Elmer Travis, Bob Thorne, and Deefy Hunt of Big B, worked on the grave from sunup until it was finished. They evened the walls straight down for five feet, squared the corners, and sought the shade when it was all over. Each man made a cigarette in gloomy silence and Deefy said: "Hell of a way to wind up the celebration."

In the shop, Carus Smith and tight-lipped Slim Thatcher sawed and hammered a coffin into shape and hardly spoke at all.

In the house, Colonel Buttrick sat in the deserted parlor amid the wreckage of the party with hush and grief thick around him. Cookie leaned in the doorway, looking blankly at the opposite wall, saying nothing. Toni was in her room. She hadn't come out since retiring hours before, when the news had come.

Stormy stayed with Jerry for a long time, until she had fallen into some kind of an exhausted slumber, making little sounds that chased themselves up and down his spine like steel fingers. He was thoroughly uncomfortable and silent. He hated Walter Proctor fervently for going out like that, for putting him in so uncomfortable a position. When Jerry quieted, seemed to drift into deeper sleep, he tip-toed out of the room, walked down the hall to the living room, and met the sightless stare of old Cookie, the sunken, pondering brightness of Colonel Buttrick's regard, and sank down into a chair, feeling irritable.

Buttrick roused himself. "You don't want to put off burying

him any longer than you have to," he said. "The heat. . . ."

Stormy looked at the older man. Out of the corner of his eyes he saw Cookie's gaze drop to his face, linger a moment, then Cookie turned and went heavily back toward the kitchen.

"We'll plant him as soon's the grave's finished," Stormy said. "Are you going to read the prayers?"

Buttrick nodded. "Yes, I suppose so."

Before the last word died away, Sam Oberlin was in the doorway. He looked straight at Stormy. "He's all ready."

Stormy stood up. "Got his best duds on him . . . and everything?"

Sam nodded. "Yeah. Want me to get Slim and Carus to help haul him to the hole?"

"Not Slim," Colonel Buttrick said, arising. "He and Walt were pretty close. Use a couple of my boys, if you want."

Sam's black eyes rested briefly on Buttrick, then swung back to Stormy, heavy eyebrows raised a little. Stormy was looking dourly at the floor. "I reckon," he said. "Yeah, let's do it that way, Sam." The bold eyes came up showing deep annoyance. "Go see if the hole's ready. If it is, get him over there. I'll round up the folks."

Colonel Buttrick ran a thin hand over his jaw and heard the rasp of beard stubble. "I ought to shave," he said indecisively. Then: "Where's the Bible?"

Stormy got it, handed it to him, and went outside, hesitated in the doorway, looking back. "You bring Toni," he said. "I'll get Jerry."

The sun was high, a hot, faded brass disc that hung in the sky like some ancient medallion, when they were all gathered around the grave. Colonel Buttrick read from the Bible. He had a good voice for that, not too low, for once not brisk and sharp. The words tolled in an old-fashioned way over the assembled bare heads, filled in the moments of deep silence, and droned through the ranch sounds that came like half-heard sighs. It took less than fifteen minutes to pass Walter Proctor from the realm of the living to the mold of the grave, and when it was all over, the gravediggers remained behind to drop MVP earth on MVP's founder.

Slim walked Jerry to the house. Carus Smith and Colonel Buttrick wandered aimlessly down toward the barn. Cookie headed for the bunkhouse in a listless way, anxious to discard the too tight coat and the shoestring tie. Sam and Stormy went as far as a long, square patch of shade by the house, and stood in its coolness.

"He threw a kink into things," Stormy said shortly.

Sam looked at him mildly. "Kink? Hell, seems to me he couldn't have done you a better turn. Now it's all yours."

The blue eyes flashed. "Dammit, Sam," Stormy said passionately, "I had plans. His dying knocks them in the head . . . I think."

"What kind of plans?"

"I had it figured out that when you boys were out gathering and marking, I'd go up around Fort Burnett and see if I could find a cattle buyer."

"His dying won't stop you," Sam said, then he frowned at Stormy. "It's too early to sell yet. Still lots of green feed around . . . unless you're figuring to. . . ."

"I'm figuring," Stormy said abruptly, "to sell MVP stuff early, before the other outfits around here even begin to gather. Nothing wrong with that, is there?"

"No," Sam said thoughtfully, watching the hard face. "Only I don't see how it'll help us get rich. You said we'd. . . ."

"You'll get rich out of this. Just be patient. Right now we want an honest buyer. After that, with our contact, we'll let things develop." Stormy turned earnestly toward Sam. "I'm betting we'll be able to do this whole thing from within the law."

Sam was puzzled. He showed it when he wagged his head, when his black eyes clouded over, became perplexed. "I don't follow you at all, Stormy."

"Don't try. Just do like I say and let me do the worrying."

"All right," Sam said, but there was no power of conviction in his words. He shrugged and gazed moodily over where the riders were sweating while filling in Proctor's grave. "You still want everything to go like you said?"

"Yeah, you're foreman. You and the boys take the wagon out. Make a good showing for MVP."

"Even with Proctor dead?"

Stormy looked up swiftly. "We want money, don't we? Then do like I say, Proctor or no Proctor. When you've got all the saleable stuff, push them toward the ranch, then, if I have any luck at Burnett, we'll have them handy for a drive up there."

"All right," Sam said, grinding out his cigarette. He started to move away, but Stormy's voice stopped him.

"Help Big B get their damned wagon harnessed up." Stormy went up to the house. Toni Buttrick was alone in the shadowy parlor. When he entered, she turned to face him, green eyes dark-glowing, face and long mouth still-looking. It annoyed him, meeting her alone right then.

"They're getting your wagon ready," he said. A sardonic expression appeared fleetingly on her face. She said nothing, and he went past her, down the dark hallway to his wife's room, and entered.

Jerry was sitting slumped in a chair, face pale, heavy mouth slack, loose-looking. Her gaze lifted to his face and clung there. There was something in her expression he had seen there several times lately, a faint remoteness, an inwardness. She didn't speak and her eyes were dry and hot-looking, as though she'd been emptied of grief. He stood looking down at her. There was no well of tenderness in him, but he knew how total her grief was.

He stood like that in silence until he heard the rattle of chain harness, then he turned toward the door again, knowing the answer to his unasked question. He went out alone to see the Big B off.

From astride her horse, Toni Buttrick's gaze stayed on him. The colonel extended a hand, responded briefly to Stormy's grip, and withdrew his fingers. Carus Smith was astride a big-boned gray horse. His frank look was more self-conscious than thoughtful when it came time for him to bid MVP good bye.

Stormy watched them ride away, going in and out of the sun splashes on the crooked road, northward. Holystone and Holk Peters were off a little to one side. Slim Thatcher was behind Stormy, his weight balanced on one leg, thumbs hooked in his shell belt, eyes above the departing Big B on the brassy, faded skyline.

When the last sound died away, Stormy turned, saw Sam Oberlin striking his pants legs with his hat, knocking wagon dust off himself, and very obviously waiting for a climax from behind Slim Thatcher. It made Stormy feel stronger, seeing Sam like that.

"I reckon you fellers know Sam's foreman of MVP and that the wagon's going out again. All right, let's get rolling." He turned toward Slim with hard confidence and a little scorn showing in his look. "You might as well stay here on the ranch, Slim. Little things you can do. I'll tell you later. Now, if you want, you can help them get the wagon ready."

He left them in the sun, staring after him, went to the house and met Cookie dolorously cleaning up the parlor. Their eyes met and Stormy said: "Cookie, Sam's foreman . . . you've probably heard. He and the boys are getting the wagon ready to go out again. You're to go with them." He waited. Cookie studied the wall in smoldering silence, made no sound at all. Stormy passed on to his wife's room and found that she hadn't moved.

A flare of quick anger shot through him. He stifled it as he sat down across from her, clasped his hands in his lap, and bent forward.

"Jerry, I'm sending the wagon out again. I wasn't satisfied with the tally before." He paused, shifted his gaze under her blank stare, then spoke again. "I guess. . . ." He stopped, grunted, and straightened up. *Damn Proctor!* "I'm going to Burnett . . . ranch business . . . but I'll be back as soon as I can. Cookie'll be with the wagon, but Slim'll be around close. Wish there was another woman around to stay with you."

The gray-black eyes cleared a little. "I'm all right," she said. Then: "You didn't really know him, Stormy." That was all she said, and, after an awkward moment of waiting, Stormy left her, went back through the house and outside where the heat bit down deeply into his lungs like a burning creosote brush. He liked it; it cleared the gloom.

Over by the barn the men were working in silence. He called Slim Thatcher, watched the lean, leggy shape detach itself, and come across the yard toward him. There was a feeling of hard triumph in Stormy.

Slim stopped in the shade, squinted eyes hooded, unfriendly. The hatred between them made it easier for Stormy to outline the menial chores he wanted Slim to do while the riders were out, while he himself was in Burnett. Slim said nothing, showed nothing beyond a dark flush, and nodded. His voice was rattling dry.

"All right. Anything else?"

"Yeah, one other thing. See if you can yank Jerry out of her slump. Make her shake it off."

Slim's eyes were bullet-hard, unblinking. He looked at Stormy a long time before he nodded and turned away without speaking and went back toward the crew and the wagon.

Stormy's lips curled upward. He watched Thatcher walk away,

allowed a long stretch of yard to get between them before he, too, went down through the shimmering heat toward the wagon. He stood, stiff-legged, watching the men in their unusual silence, then went past to the barn, inside where the coolness smote him, and there he stopped when he heard his name called softly and saw Sam walking toward him.

"Yeah?"

"It looks like there's trouble coming," Sam said soberly.

Stormy lifted his saddle down from its peg. He shot Sam a look and said: "I reckon you'll know how to handle it, if it does."

Sam watched him hang the rig on his hip. "And what if they all quit?"

"Let them. Maybe we'd be better off with new hands anyway. They've all got loyalty to MVP as it was . . . not as it is now and as it's going to be from now on."

Sam shuffled his feet and scowled. "Not on a roundup, dammit," he said.

"Sure, any time they want to. If they throw a little kink into us, we'll get over it. Proctor threw us one and I'm going to Burnett anyway. Hell, Burnett'll have plenty of riders hanging around if we need new ones."

But Sam's notions weren't so direct. He still scowled. The scar on his face shone with sweat. He swore softly. "They don't say anything. Work like a bunch of damned mutes."

"So long as they work," Stormy said. "Who's sparking it . . . Slim?"

"Naw, it isn't one man, it's all of them. And Holystone gives me the creeps. Him and his damned medicine bundle."

Stormy smiled, thinking there was enough Indian in Sam to give him this vulnerable spot of superstition. The saddle grew heavy. He started for the doorway and the corral beyond. "Those are the things a foreman's got to put up with, Sam," he said. "Don't let it throw you. If they get troublesome, fire the passel of them."

He left Sam in the barn, looking after him, saddled up his black horse, stepped across him, and jogged out of the yard without looking back. Four sets of eyes followed him.

# CHAPTER FIFTEEN

The way he sat the saddle, held the reins, and carried himself spelled out a confidence that had always lain close beneath the surface of his hardness. He rode boldly, a strong and confident man crossing his own domain.

He came to one of the nearly straight places in the dusty old road, all mottled and weary under the leaching sun blast, and lifted the black horse into an easy lope. Shady coolness alternated with patches of burnished heat to press against him. Overhead a faded sky of purest blue hung, passive, patient, waiting for an end to another blistering summer day. He rode with a keen singing in his heart and a feeling that the entire world was Marais Valley and that it was his or would be very shortly. The upthrusting hills on either side of the valley seemed to squat, to hunker down and press their bony flanks hard upon the rich valley floor, searching for the pleasant drafts of lazy air that were so cool and humid down here.

At the end of the day, or at least when he came to the little creek and camping spot where he and Jerry Proctor had found love, he slung his saddle down, draped the blanket to dry, and hobbled the black horse. From a saddlebag he took out some paper-wrapped meat and, squatting near the creek in the shade, ate, and watched the shadows come, the long, bloody wave of twilight fall. He saw a flash of brilliant black and white feathers wheel in from the heights for a roosting spot. A magpie. His right hand dipped and fell, lifted in a blur of movement, and the silence was shattered by the shot. The magpie seemed to come apart in a burst of feathers. It fell in the underbrush, hung there, long tail quivering.

He finished eating, drank at the creek, cleaned and re-loaded his gun, held it in his hand a long time, hefting it, then slid it back into the holster, and lay back with the long-running spillways of light slanting down across the glade. He didn't see the solitary horseman who appeared on a lip of a hill eastward. Drawn by the gunshot, the man sat there for a long time, eyes searching for movement, and when he saw the hobbled black horse, he sat a while longer, recognizing the animal, then rode back down the far side of the hill, out of sight.

The night was warm and Stormy slept uncovered, flat on the grass with the murmur of the creek in his mind. When he awoke, it was fragrantly dark. The milky array of stars was distant, unmoving, aloof in their black heavens. He caught the horse, saddled up, and rode northward. He pushed the animal as long as it was cool and was nearing Fort Burnett when the sun finally lumbered from behind western ramparts, balanced for a moment, long enough to pour a great gushing torrent of heat and stark brilliance down over the land, then lifted higher, higher.

Fort Burnett was awake and stirring when Stormy put up his horse, ate a stringy breakfast, and sat under the overhang near the Central Valley Saloon and watched the people, sluggish with heat lethargy. The sharpness was back in his eyes, the wolfish look of a hunted man.

It had been a long time since he had felt like he did now. There was excitement and anxiety and caution, violent readiness, all meshed together inside him, a potent elixir that filled him from instinctive sources. The fiery torment every outlaw felt when danger was close; it was fear and dare compounded, and he reveled in it.

Freighters trooped in and out of the beaneries. A few riders were in town. Squaws and tame Indians, dejected, bedraggled, smelling of mutton fat, stale whiskey, and sour sweat, took up places in the shade. A musty odor of manure and dust was rank when traffic stirred the roadway, and somewhere, north and east of town, cattle were lowing their dry-rattling plea for water. Stormy got up, satisfied with what he'd seen of the town's lassitude, and strolled toward the noise.

He passed the Drover's Union where a tall, bronzed man was emerging from the hotel door, and went on by. The bronzed man stopped still in his tracks, looking after him. There was a quick intentness in the stranger's face. His eyes followed Stormy's figure with its soft-slapping ivory-butted gun. The stranger stood rooted. He wore a long black coat that hung to his hips. It lay open and beneath was a heavy shell belt that sagged. The cloth bulged thickly where a gun rode beneath the coat. The man's hat was small, stiff-brimmed, and flat-topped. Beneath it was a shock of stiff auburn hair with a hint of gray over the ears. The cheek bones were high, prominent, the nose straight, predatory-looking, the mouth thin, uncompromising. It was the stillness of the eyes, though, that held a strangeness, for they never moved or seemed to waver or doubt as they clung to Stormy's retreating back. Finally the man turned north on the hard walk, strolled in the same direction Stormy had taken.

The cattle smell came first, then the sight of a patched, bleached-out old pole corral of generous size, and finally, the dull, scruffy coats of heat-rusted animals.

Stormy swung over by the chutes where some men lounged without shade. He got close enough to hear their talk while he looked through the poles at the slab-sided, tongue-lolling cattle. Their great horns shone wickedly; their eyes were red, dry, and looked long-suffering. There was trail dust on them. While he gazed at the cattle, he also measured the three men. One was tall, as scrawny and wild-looking as the longhorns. Stormy

132

guessed him to be the owner. Cowman was stamped forever in his bearing, his squint, and his speech. On either side of him the others stood. They were buyers. One was fatter than the other; aside from that they might have been brothers. The lean Texan between them seemed to weigh each sound carefully. One of the buyers was sucking on a soggy, unlit cigar. He had a buggy whip in his fist that he repeatedly poked through the corral at the animals. "There," he said contemptuously. "There's one. See him? Won't weigh six-fifty wringing wet. Jeezuz. Feller get a mouthful of him . . . the longer he'd chew the bigger it'd get."

The Texan looked and said nothing. The other buyer spat, regarded his expectoration briefly, then looked back at the cattle. Tiredly he said: "Got to give 'em water. They got a shrink on 'em you could read a newspaper through." He patently wasn't interested in the animals for his gaze wandered to Stormy, took in the ivory-butted gun, the square jaw and strong set of shoulders, and flickered with bored interest. He took his leg off the bottom pole and turned away. "See you fellers," he said, and started away.

The Texan stared at the thin, thirsty cattle like he was mesmerized by them. He didn't speak. Then he pushed away from the corral, strolled after the departing buyer, and went past a tall man in a frock coat who was watching him from the shade of a nearby corral. He caught up with the buyer and swung into step beside him.

"Buy you a drink, mister."

The buyer looked around, showed no surprise, and said, "Sure. Maybe it'll be cold."

They entered the Central Valley Saloon and bellied up to the bar. When the beer came, the buyer hung a foot on the rail and peered at Stormy over the rim of his glass. "You got cattle to sell?" he said.

"Yeah."

"Well," the buyer said, setting the glass down carefully, "I'm going to tell you something, pardner . . . if they aren't strong and in good flesh don't drive 'em to Burnett."

"They're better'n the ones you were looking at in the corral."

The buyer made a face. "If they aren't," he said dryly, "then they're dead and won't lie down." The man's disillusioned eyes went to the beer glass and the little rim of moisture around its base. "Market's not bad right now but hell . . ."—he made a weary gesture with one hand—"you fellers've all got the same problem . . . thin cattle." The eyes came up. "When are you going to learn to upgrade your animals? You're trying to compete with Indianans and Michiganders and y'just can't do it. They feed cattle corn, them dirt farmers. Their critters're ten times as good as Texas beef."

"We'll upgrade in time," Stormy said, signaling for two more beers. "Right now I want to know if it'll pay me to drive in early with a grassed-out herd."

A long silence, then a sigh. "Grassed-out to you," the cattle buyer said, "but you fellers always see your critters a lot better'n we do. Honestly now . . . can you see ribs on them?"

"No."

"Have they got enough grease on 'em to stand the drive? If bones show after they get to Burnett, it's no good."

"I can get them here without any bones showing. It'll take a little longer."

"Take all the damned time you want," the buyer said. "Ranchers, once they get a drive going, seem to think they're racing the devil. Scared there'll be other herds ahead of them. Well . . . what's the difference? If you drive in good critters, you can be the last man in and still get the best price." The buyer drank off his second beer with an air of resignation on his perspiring face. "There ain't no hurry, pardner. Fat's what the market wants

. . . not speed."

Stormy set his glass aside. "These are MVP cattle," he said, and watched for reaction.

A little life showed in the buyers' eyes. It died out almost at once. "Walt Proctor's stuff." The eyes went up to Stormy's face again, studying it. "Walt's stuff usually comes in lean. Where's Slim? He come up with you?"

"No, Walter Proctor's dead. We buried him yesterday."

"The hell," he said softly.

"And Slim's not foreman any more. A man named Sam Oberlin is."

The buyer's eyes grew round suddenly. "By God," he said in the same soft way. "You must . . . I heard Walt's daughter got married."

Stormy nodded. "To me," he said.

"Oh." The buyer's lethargy fell away. He painstakingly rubbed one damp palm on his paunch and held out the hand. "I'm Al Gregory," he said.

"Merrill," Stormy said. "Glad to know you."

They shook and the buyer's nod was thoughtful. "Me, too. Is MVP going to drive in early this year?"

"Yeah. I have an idea that coming in before the fall rush will bring us better prices."

"It will," Gregory said firmly. "Sure it will. Now then, if you bring in *fat* cattle, you'll do even better'n market . . . with early stuff. I've been buying here at Fort Burnett for six years, preaching my lungs out for fat cattle . . . and what do I get? Same damned trail-shrunk critters every time. It makes you sick." He motioned for another brace of beers. "Know what, Merrill? One of these days there won't be any market for Texas cattle. Mark my word. Those Eastern farmers'll skim off the cream and you fellers'll be sucking the hind teat like orphan calves. I know." He flipped a coin on the bar, leaned sideways, and sipped his beer, looking over at Stormy. "Texas has got too many cattle and not enough quality in them. Oh, hell . . . for now, sure . . . you can sell 'em because the Yankee states are beef-starved, but it isn't always going to be that way . . . bank on it, Merrill . . . it isn't always going to be that way."

Stormy listened and thought and drank beer, then he smiled and set the empty glass aside. "That's all I rode up here to find out," he said. "Now I'll go back and make up a herd and trail them in." The smile died slowly from his face. Gregory's black eyes were sharp-looking, shrewd. "I reckon if I bring them in fat and topped-out, you'll be interested in them."

Gregory bobbed his head. "Plenty interested. If you can do that, you and me'll team up any time you've got something to sell." The buyer paused, licked his lips. "Too bad about Walt," he said, "but y'know . . . Walt was like all of them. You couldn't tell him how to top off his cattle. I hope you're different."

"I am," Stormy said, and left the buyer at the bar, crossed the room, and shouldered past the doors, stood in the shade a moment, then went toward the livery barn through the dust of the roadway on a diagonal route.

A tall man, sitting on a bench, watched him cross the road, then got up and entered the saloon, went up to the bar, and hung his arms over it next to Al Gregory. Without more than a glance at the buyer he said: "How's the cow business?"

Gregory sized up the stranger. Only in a general way did he look to be a cowman. Gregory shrugged. "It might get better one of these days. When Texas cowmen learn what's going to happen to Texas cattle if they don't change their ways."

The stranger turned sideways with his beer in his hand, reached up, and thumbed back his hat. His prominent cheek bones made shadows for the clear eyes to lie in. "That feller you were just talking to . . . is he a cowman from hereabouts?"

"From MVP down in Marais Valley." Gregory recited a little

of MVP's history.

"Well," the lean man said, "that makes him an owner then, don't it?"

"I expect so." Gregory's dark eyes grew thoughtful. "Seems like a sharp feller, too. Interested in better prices and upgrading MVP stock. That's what Texas needs, better cowmen."

"What's his name?"

"Name? Oh . . . Merrill. I didn't catch the first name."

The stranger looked startled. "Merrill," he repeated. "I'll be damned. His right name."

"What?"

"Merrill," the stranger said again. There was an odd light in his eyes. "Well, thanks."

He left Al Gregory at the bar and went back out into the heat smash, stood well back in the shadows, and looked southward where a rider was passing through shimmering heat waves, an ivory-butted gun moving rhythmically with the shuffling walk of his black horse. The sere country around Fort Burnett, scorched, pale, bloodless, and gasping, made sickly contrast to the sheen of the black horse and its rider.

Stormy passed beyond the farthest hovels that hung like broken teeth far down the roadway, out onto the cowed plain that lay southward, to the undulating little hills and swales beyond where lay the drop-off into Marais Valley. He was in no hurry—no hurry at all—so when he came to the trail leading homeward he followed it as far as the jutting buttes above Big B, and there he spent the night near a sump spring where mosquitoes went into ecstasies after darkness came, and he finally had to hide himself in a thicket to avoid them.

Before sunup he was moving again, as far as a shadowed cleft in the rolling land, watching the thin, perfectly erect smoke rise above the Buttrick kitchen chimney. He was still there three hours later, as patient as any Indian, smoking, back to the tree where he'd tied the black horse. And he saw her go out, go to the barn, saddle up, and ride off due east. Then he squashed the cigarette, got up with slitted eyes, humming a broken tune, tugged up his cinch, got astride, and also rode due east. He stayed back out of sight for a while, then dropped down a little where the land dipped southward.

She was still riding. Close enough to make out the details, he recognized the horse—the ewe-necked one he'd ridden into Marais Valley months before. The bold smile came up.

When she was three miles east of the home place, he topped out over a blunt hill where talus rock lay, wind-whipped, got a tall old tree behind him to negate the skylining effect, and plotted her course in his mind. A study of the landfall showed where a water hole, purple and inviting with shade, lay directly in her path. He swung the black horse toward it, lifted him into a lope, and rode a big circle to get there ahead of her. When he dismounted, he hobbled the animal, slipped off its bridle, hung it on the saddle horn, and loosened the cinch.

When she came swinging up, he was lying full length, hat carelessly thrown aside, smoking and looking beyond her at the solitary spindrift of long, thin clouds that lay peaceful on the shimmering horizon.

She pulled her horse in sharply, sat there staring at him. "This isn't Wednesday," she finally said, almost fiercely.

He laughed at her. "Sure isn't, is it? Get down."

She didn't dismount, but leaned a little, looking down at him. "What are you doing here, Stormy?"

"On my way back from Burnett. Saw you riding and waited for you. Any harm in that?" He let the bold smile drop down long enough to sweep over the horse. "He looks better'n when I had him." Then he chuckled. "Big B's good to its animals. I've noticed that."

She got down. He watched her care for the horse, hobble and

turn it loose, slip off the bridle, fling it carelessly over the horn, then walk slowly into the shade near him and sink down.

He had never seen her look anything but confident, arrogant. Today she appeared troubled. The green eyes were pensive and rebellious-looking, the long mouth set in a stubborn line that was unbecoming. He leaned on an elbow, studying her, evolving slow, cold thoughts about her, playing with her image like he'd play with a wounded wolf.

"What's the matter, Toni?"

"Matter!" She spat it out, looked fiercely at him and away. "The matter is Carus."

"Oh." He was mildly amused at her vehemence. "I reckon I'll guess. He wants to marry you."

"That," she said spitefully, "isn't anything new. Now my father's taking a hand."

His smile faded a little, got hung up on the bones of his face, and didn't quite leave but lost all its shape. He looked thoughtfully calculating, hard.

She said: "Walter Proctor's death is responsible. It scared Dad. He wants to see me married to Carus just in case. . . ." She turned fully toward him. There was bitterness in her voice. "Like you're married to Geraldine. Damn her . . . no, not her . . . you. Damn you, Stormy!"

Something in him responded to her savage mood. It was shady, it was secluded, and fragrant in the bower by the water hole and she, angry, resentful, her slimness drawn erect, her long mouth thrust out in rebellion, fired him. He reached for her and she went to him with surprising ease and willingness. He hadn't thought she would be like that, not with her emotions, her anger aroused, but she was, and he decided it was one of the facets of her personality—the strangeness that made her so interesting to him. In the back of his mind moved an idea, the same idea he'd had at Cap-Rock Spring when last they'd been together. It centered around Carus Smith, handsome, naïve, cuckolded, total damned fool.

The bold scorn died out when he kissed her, the lids fell, and his breath was dammed up behind his lips, waiting, waiting.

She moved, groped in blind suddenness for his neck, pulled him down closer, harder, the rapture of pain burning like flame in her. He responded and high overhead a great, whirling buzzard looked down, cocked an ugly, unclean head, and saw them there. Its sweeping sight saw something else, too—a harassed man, riding eastward slowly, bent from the waist, studying the ground, following the tracks of Toni's horse with an anxious look on his face. A young man in whose heart there was an iron core of pain that was an echo of words Colonel Buttrick had said to him: *You've got to do what must be done, Carus. I'm at my wits' end.*

She pulled free of Stormy, sat up, green eyes big and round with something inexplicable, whirling, writhing in their depths, and she drew back a hand and struck him across the face, twice. He was jarred each time. The surging blood roared in his ears. He caught her hand and forced it down, back. She grunted. He forced her down until she fell back, staring at him with agony dark in her eyes. "Why'd you do that, you hellcat?"

Her answer came thinly, unevenly. "Because you'll go back to *her* and when you come again it'll be from *her.*"

He let go her arm quickly, bent low. "Sure," he said savagely, "and I'll come back because of you . . . because of green eyes and a lot of other things, but I'll come back and that's what counts."

He took her roughly, hurting her, bending her against him, and feeling for her mouth and the high-soaring buzzard dipped a little to see what must happen. The horseman was getting closer, but there were still primitive moments to be lived.

Toni and Stormy lived them until she wrenched away and

leaped up, long mouth twisted, green eyes swimming. She ran to her horse, slipped the bridle on, leaped aboard, and dug in her spurs so that the animal made a wild lunge and lit in a belly-down run, blindly eastward. A wild cry trailed in her wake.

Stormy watched her go. There was anger and cruelty in his expression, then he, too, arose, caught his own horse, and rode away from the spring, but southward toward MVP. When Carus Smith came up the glade, he was livid with invisible tension, but there was no one there—only tracks, torn grass, and low, where he couldn't see it, the salt-drying specks where tears had been flung down.

Carus dismounted slowly, stood at his horse's head, face pinched up and held in a quandary, trying to sort out the sign all around him of what had happened. A half-breed like Sam Oberlin would have read it all in an instant and laughed. Holystone would have known, too, for he'd seen that sign before in the path of Stormy Merrill, but Carus Smith only partly read it and his mind wouldn't interpret it right, so he finally wheeled his horse and struck out eastward, patiently, tirelessly following the girl's tracks.

Stormy went south with the sun burning hot against his ribs, down one leg, and high on his head through the dark dampness of his hat. In his mind a surfeited hotness lay.

He shuffled onto the road and let the black horse have its head. He was home. From beneath his hat brim raking eyes saw the yard. It was clean. That pleased and amused him. He rode to the barn, unsaddled, and turned the black horse out. The ranch was huddled in a stillness of late midday all its own. He stood back in the shade and made a cigarette, smoked it, saw how the place looked with the rubbish piles gone, the cast-offs hauled away. Even the scraggly old rosebush was trimmed. His eyes pinpointed on that. Slim must have taken hours to do that, on the gallery; maybe Jerry had been there with him, talking as he worked. He strangled the cigarette and went slowly across the heat-lashed yard into the house and down the hall. She wasn't there.

He went out to the kitchen. Cookie looked up, startled, then mumbled something, and turned away. A caving-in sensation behind Stormy's belt made his voice sound hollow.

"What the hell are you doing here, Cookie?"

"Me?" Cookie said, his back to Stormy. "I just came back . . . that's what I'm doing here. They didn't need me with the wagon. Holystone's cooking for them."

Stormy went closer, reached out with a claw-like hand, gripped the old man's shoulder, and forced him around. Their faces were very close. "Cookie," he said in his too-gentle way, "*I say when you're to come back. Understand me? I say!* When I say you're to go out with the wagon, by God you're to *stay* out with it."

Wild hell showed in the depths of Cookie's eyes. His old mouth quivered behind its drooping mustache, and big, mottled fists bunched up. Stormy's hand dropped away, his eyes bored hotly. "Why did you leave them? Who said for you to?"

"No one said for me to. I come in because of . . . her. She needs someone around right now. It ain't ri—"

"Cookie," Stormy said very quietly, "Proctor's dead. You may have been an old hand with him. With me you're just Cookie, that's all. You don't think, you don't do a damned thing you aren't told to do. Get that through your head. There won't be any next time . . . remember that. Now get a horse and get back to the wagon."

He left the room with wrath lying coiled in his belly, the icily directed logic of it as clear, as sharply defined and stark in his mind as it could be, and when he pushed out through the door into the gallery and saw them riding in—his wife and Slim Thatcher—the fires burned low.

He waited in the shadow of the big rosebush until they had finished with their barn chores. As they were walking across the yard, he stepped out to face them. Slim's eyes, squinted tight, were hidden, but Jerry's gaze leaped to his face and hung there. She said something in a small, brief way, and Slim veered off, went around toward the back of the house without speaking. She stepped up into the shade with its soft fragrance and stood before him.

"I'm glad you're back, Stormy." She said it simply, without inflection, as though she were facing a necessity, but not a pleasure.

"Are you?" The blue eyes bled a peculiar, dead wave at her. "Slim didn't seem to be."

"Stormy." She touched his hand, let her fingers trail away, went around him to a bench, and sank down. "Stormy . . . please, don't torture him any more. Not Slim. At least let him ride with the others."

"He doesn't have to stay. There's lots of Texas beyond these hills."

She looked down at her hands. "Man hate is a terrible thing. Why do you hate him so?"

"Hate him? I don't hate him. I just don't think he's much of a cowman, that's all, and MVP's got no room for anything but cowmen . . . from here on."

"Stormy? Sit down beside me, won't you?"

Something stirred within him. Studying her, he thought there was something unusually poignant about her. Without speaking, he perched on the gallery railing where her father had stood that last night. "Well?" he said, watching the long, black lift of eyelashes sweep upward until her eyes were on his face.

"Stormy . . . I understand, a little. I couldn't say it right the day you left, but I think I can now. It's you . . . what you are . . . that makes you unable to feel . . . sometimes."

"What the hell kind of talk is that?" he said, frowning a little.

"You didn't understand after Dad died. That's all, you just didn't understand that people stay close to one another when that happens." She searched his face. "That's what I meant. It isn't really very important, I don't suppose, but I wanted you to know. . . ."

He squirmed on the railing, looking steadily at her. When he spoke, the anger was gone and in its place wariness. "I did that wrong, didn't I?" His eyes wavered, went to the edge of the house, and hardened when he remembered the way Slim had walked around there, without looking at him, without speaking. "That's what's eating him, too, isn't it?"

"Nothing is eating him, Stormy. I've got something else to tell you." She twined her fingers together. "Maybe this isn't the time, though."

He swung back toward her and uneasiness stirred. "What? Now's as good a time as any. What is it?"

She stood up, took two steps, and was close to him, close enough for him to catch the fragrance of her. "You're going to be a father, darling." For just a moment she stood there, almost swaying toward him, then she spun in a blur of movement and was gone.

He looked after her dumbly, heard the faint sound as the door closed, and felt something like lead deep within himself.

He was still perched there when the sound of spurs around the corner of the house snagged at his mind and made him turn to look. Slim was walking, head down, beside Cookie, whose stumping gait wasn't helped any by the load of things he carried, wrapped in a huge old white cloth. Both men kept their heads averted.

Stormy slid off the railing. When his boots struck the gallery floor, the spurs made a strident, musical sound. Neither man looked around. It was as though he wasn't there or didn't exist.

Anger returned and burned in his throat. He watched them cross the yard slowly, disappear into the maw of the old barn, then he swore.

The mood lasted until long after twilight. Jerry called him from within the house. He entered, lit a lamp on a parlor table, and went toward the kitchen. She met him with a strange, haunted gaze. He turned toward the long table. There were only two places set there.

He sluiced off out back, dried his face and hands on a roller towel, and went back inside. She was sitting very straight-backed, waiting for him. He sat down and they began to eat. It was an awkward meal, and when it was over, he stood up.

"Leave the dishes," he said, "and let's take a walk."

Her still features grew suddenly alive, animated. She threw the apron aside and went through the back door with him. The night was down, soft and full, and, as they walked aimlessly through the scented grass, weariness welled up within him, spread in an exhausted, pleasurable way to the very extremities of his being. He had used himself hard that day.

When they were far enough away so that the buildings were lost in the shroud of night, he stopped, turned, looking down at her. A strange and ghostly phosphorescence illuminated her, seemed to limn her against the dark vault she stood in.

Slowly he said: "Congratulations, Jerry." It wasn't the right thing and he knew it; it was an effort in the right direction, and he also knew that.

She smiled up at him and the uncertainty, the doubt that had lain across her face since his return—and for days before—was erased. "You could kiss me," she said.

He did, and she turned back his slow ardor with a fierce zeal that seemed to burst inside his head, leave the stain of passion on his lips.

"It'll be a boy, won't it, Stormy?"

"Yeah, it ought to be."

"Could we call him Walter?"

"Sure," he said. "Sit down."

She sank down on the hard earth, waiting, but he didn't have anything to say and a breath of regret, of the old uncertainty, passed over her face like a shadow.

"Stormy . . . you aren't disappointed in me?"

He looked around at her, scarcely comprehending. "Disappointed? No, why should I be? Oh, *that?* No, I think that's fine."

"Do you really?" The words gushed, ran together, erupted in a burst of breath that was sweet on his face.

"Sure," he said, reaching for her. "A boy named Walter Stormy Merrill."

She lay back with him in passive silence. For a long time he was motionless. Through his tiredness a lot of threads were weaving themselves into a pattern of odd design. The cattle drive he must organize and supervise, the knotty, unresolved problem of mastery of Marais Valley, of Big B. And nearer, more vivid, the memory of Toni—the way she had slapped him in an excess of passion, of how she'd surrendered, and the way she'd fled with a wild cry. And unbidden came the image of Slim Thatcher. His lips curled. Slim would understand; he'd know how to be gentle, tender; he'd know the right things to say to Jerry. He rolled over and raised himself on one arm, looked down at the shiny black hair and the heavy mouth, at the gray-black eyes that were fully on him in a somber and deeply troubling way.

"Where were you and Slim when I rode in?"

"We went for a ride over by the moss tank. Why?"

"Nothing."

She lifted an arm, put her fingers on the jut of his jaw, worked them up so softly he scarcely felt them, to his cheeks, on up into his hair, then let the fingers fall away.

"Stormy, are you jealous?"

His laugh was hard. "Of Slim? Sooner be jealous of Holy-stone." A glowing brilliance lay in his gaze. "He'd make you a second father, never a husband. Not enough fire in him for you, Jerry."

Softly she said: "Darling, he's been at MVP since I was a little girl."

"I know. He's a fixture. All right, he can stay. I haven't anything special against him, but, Jerry, we want Marais Valley to grow rich, don't we?"

"If you do," she said, watching the hard play of expression in his face, "I do, too."

He smiled at her. "I'll *make* it grow rich."

# Chapter Sixteen

He didn't meet Toni the following Wednesday because he was at the wagon twelve miles away with Holk Peters, Holystone, and Sam. With his coming, a discreet silence descended even around the cooking fire that Cookie tended sullenly as they all read the tally sheets, a time-honored moment when every rider gave at least one opinion. Sam had a small twig, which he kept stabbing into the ground. He leaned upon it briefly, and sat back again, making a row of shallow holes. His face was thinner-looking, the shiny scar more livid.

Little twinings of fire arose and sent out smells of grease-wood. Stormy handed the tally sheets back to Sam and looked around. Holystone was rocking himself back and forth, just barely, like a Comanche seeking a vision. Holk Peters was as still as a log, as square and shapeless. Cookie's snuffling, his shuffling old gait over by the chuck wagon tailboard, sounded loud in the star-washed night. A new moon, as thin and wicked-looking as a curved dagger, shed weak light.

"Well," Stormy said, looking at Holk Peters, but addressing them all, "I reckon that's that. We can start for home in the morning."

Holystone stopped rocking, his eyes wide open and fastened on Stormy's face. "A good gather," he said.

"Yeah, better'n before."

Holystone's eyes didn't leave Stormy's face when Stormy turned aside, to look at Sam Oberlin. "We'll take them to the ranch. In a day or two we'll cut back the real young stuff, the cows and bulls."

"Make up a drive?" Sam asked.

"Yeah."

Holystone's gaze sharpened. "Early, ain't it?" he said. "We usually don't drive till fall. Sometimes after the First of October."

"This time we're going in early," Stormy said. "I just got back from Burnett. The market's good right now."

"We could make more weight if we waited," Holystone persisted, not liking the idea of departing from custom.

"What good's the weight if it's all bone and horn?" Stormy said. "And when you've gotten up there in past years you had just that to sell. Bones and horns. We're going to drift them easy, Holystone. Get 'em to Fort Burnett without a rib showing."

Holystone absorbed this without speaking. He looked down into the winking eye of the fire.

Sam got up and spat out a cigarette stub. Stormy stood up, also. They walked out where the rope corral was and only Holk Peters didn't look after them. In a bitter, soft way Cookie said: "MVP's never done nothing right up till now."

Out where the smell of horses was strong, Stormy and Sam stopped. The half-breed began without preamble. "We made a hell of a good showing, Stormy. I believe you was righter than you knew."

"How do you mean?"

"About Slim. Christ . . . we gathered close to a hundred and eighty head he never even found."

"Honest stuff?" Stormy asked, surprised.

"Yep." The dark eyes glowed. "And I've been thinking. I got close to another hundred head of slicks for MVP. I ought to get a slice off that, hadn't I?"

"Sure, and you will. In fact, I'll give it to you now, if you want it."

Sam's teeth shone in the darkness. "I'll wait until we sell," he said drawlingly. "You might under-guess the market. Well, anyway, I like the sound of this, Stormy."

"Stay by me," Stormy said. "Just stay by me, Sam. You'll come out 'way ahead."

"I'm beginning to believe it," Sam said. "Now then, I reckon you want to know how the crew made out."

But Stormy shook his head. "To hell with the crew," he said. "I know Cookie went back. The rest of them seem all right. At least they're talking again. What I want to know is . . . did any of them think you might be picking up slicks?"

Sam shook his head. "Naw. I did that on my own when I'd ride out from them."

"All right," Stormy said. "Now you can drift them back to MVP."

"Nothing to that. And if a few Big B cows trail along, no one'll think anything about it. We always have some Big Bs in our gathers. Where it'll get ticklish is when we cut 'em out. You and me had better do that. I'll send the boys out cleaning water holes. We can shape up the drive, push the cut-backs a day's drive from home, then the drive'll be long gone when the old cows come bawling around. Anyway, I just picked up big weaned stuff. No cows will bag up. How's it sound?"

"Good," Stormy said. He thought that Sam hadn't been able to resist a little rustling; it amused him. "Anything else?"

"Not a hell of a lot. Cookie left, and when he returned, I knew you were back at the ranch. He was sorer'n a cut calf but kept it to himself. Him and Holystone're getting awful thick."

"No real trouble like you thought there might be?"

"Naw. I reckon keeping Slim away took the guts out of them." The dark eyes were thoughtfully steady. "By the way . . . how is

Slim? He quit yet?"

"No, and I don't think he ever will, either."

Sam killed his cigarette. "Carus Smith rode in a couple days ago."

"Yeah?"

"He was pretty quiet." Sam's shoulders lifted and fell. "It wasn't anything about us. I watched him. He had something on his mind and it wasn't cattle." A quick smile. "I could've stolen twenty head right in front of him and he wouldn't have noticed."

"What was it . . . his trouble?"

"Damned if I know. He ate, drank some coffee, mooned around, then rode on back toward home. I trailed him a ways." Sam grunted. "He never even looked back."

"I think I know what was eating him. Well, Sam, roll them for home at sunup."

"Just a second. Did you mean it when you said we'd drive 'em slow and get to Burnett without a shrink?"

"Every word of it, why?"

"I just wondered," Sam said. "I never liked slow drives."

"No one else does, either, but we're going to take our time. You'll see why when we get paid off."

They went back to the camp, saw the mounds that were men, and bedded down themselves. For a long time Stormy didn't sleep, and when he did, he didn't sleep long. He was the first one up and had Cookie's fire cracking and spitting with new life before the cook came out of his bedroll under the wagon. They exchanged a quick, unavoidable stare, an infinitesimal nod of heads, and Stormy went out to the rope corral, caught his horse, saddled him, and led him back to the stirring camp.

"Sam."

The half-breed came over, stood hip-shot, waiting.

"I'm going upcountry a ways. You don't need me anyway. When I get home, we'll make up our herd for the drive."

"All right," Sam said. "Tomorrow."

Stormy rode through the peaceful valley with the sunlight falling just ahead of him. He found an ancient trail faint upon the ground and followed its meanderings, saw how it detoured with studied frequency, swinging to hilltops then falling back down off them again, and knew it was an old, old Indian road. In the morning's daylight he let the valley's atmosphere of peace and quiet seep into him, make him relaxed and comfortable.

Coming abruptly over a land swell whose gentle terminus lay where a creek ate at its banks, he was joined in the cathedral silence by a raucous and flashing blue jay that flew excitedly ahead of him, giving the eternal cry of all blue jays, warning animals that a man was approaching. He felt the cool ivory of his gun butt, but didn't draw the weapon. A peculiar lethargy was upon him. The stone-boldness of his glance had softened. He laughed at himself. Marais Valley did that to a man—buried him under layers of beauty and peacefulness threatening never to let him rise up out of them again. He took his hand away from the gun, made a cigarette, lit it, and kept the sun along his right side, feeling very much at peace with himself and his world until he thought of his destination. Then the mellowness died from his expression, the brief touch of peacefulness from his eyes. It wasn't enough to ride through this; a man had to own it, all of it, and in order to do that. . . .

A solitary horseman topped out on a ridge off to his left, and the old swift-curdling anxiety shot through him, snuffing out everything but primitive alertness. The rider watched Stormy for a long time, then he whirled his horse, went along the skyline as far as a dip in the hill, which debouched via an arroyo to the valley floor, followed down it, and booted his horse into a lope as soon as he hit flat ground, in a direct line toward Stormy.

Nearby were some trees. Stormy rode that far, reined up, and sat there, watching, waiting. Close enough, he recognized the slimness, the suppleness of Toni Buttrick. He was momentarily pleased for it saved him having to wait her out like he'd done before. She had been his destination. Then he grew thoughtful, watching her come up. Why was she hanging around the country where MVP's crew was making its second gather? When she pulled down to a walk and cut into the shade, let the reins swing, and stared hard at him with a faintly flushed face and unusually bright and glassy-looking eyes, he was frowning at her.

"You're quite a ways from home," he said, when she stopped her horse. "And out early, too."

"I've got to talk to you, Stormy."

"Sure, but how'd you know where I was?"

"I've been riding everywhere, every day, looking for you. And . . . Carus is following me."

Instinctively Stormy studied the horizon, the escarpment he'd first seen her come down. There was nothing there. She dismounted, and led her horse closer to him. He'd never seen her look so small, so frightened and unsure before. With a grunt he swung down beside her.

"Why's Carus following you?"

"He followed me that day . . . the last time we met, over by the water hole."

The blue eyes grew still and thoughtful. After a moment he said: "Damned good thing he was slow getting up there."

She reached out, took his arm, and bit down hard with her fingers. "Stormy. . . ."

"What's wrong with you, Toni?" He peeled the fingers away with his free hand, scowled down at her harshly.

She dropped her reins and fell against him. Reluctantly he closed his arms around her, felt her quake from sobs, and forced her head back. Her lids were closed, the green eyes hidden. In a strangling way she told him and he was too startled to move for a long time, then he held her off gently and looked down into her flushed, contorted face.

She read the disbelief in his expression and her mouth became twisted and ugly. "You don't believe me, do you? You. . . ."

"Hold on a minute," he said. "Just a minute." He saw the flooding wildness of her look, knew how she responded to his touch when she was emotionally torn this way, and the thought was unpleasant to him.

"Are you sure, Toni?" She nodded. "All right," he said hastily. "All right. Calm down. Get hold of yourself."

It made his mind ice-clear. Jerry at home, and now Toni. He was lost in thought a moment, his mind fastening on the secret scheme. Well, here it was . . . what he'd planned with brutal, harsh calculation. He looked at her differently now.

"You've got to marry Carus. There's no other way." It was so easy to tell her that.

She looked like he'd struck her, eyes wild, face ashen, lips lying, loose and open. "Carus?" It was a whisper. "Carus? You. . . . You. . . !"

Sharply he said: "Is there any other way?"

"Yes, we could run away."

"You're crazy," he said. "That's impossible. Listen to me . The only way we can salvage what we've got is for you to marry Carus. Dammit, Toni, running would only make it worse."

Solid, convincing arguments rushed to his mind. Marais Valley ownership was in jeopardy; he had anticipated this moment and it thrilled him to fight her, to bend every effort to make her do as he wished, as he'd planned in the dark, secret place in his mind that had led him to this crucial point in their relationship—in his scheme to rule her and, through her, the upper half of the valley.

"If we ran away, could I marry you? I couldn't and you know

it, but you've got to have a husband. Use your head. Carus is the only way out for both of us."

They stood almost toe to toe, the air around them vibrating with a tight and terrible breathlessness. She said nothing. There was a stricken look in her green eyes, an abandoned slackness to her long mouth.

He talked on, feeling his way with words, thinking aloud, formulating, trying mightily to lead her along through the dilemma he'd so patently led her into. Far back in his consciousness was a shouting cry that this must be as he'd planned it, that she *had* to do as he said.

When he stopped speaking, she was moving away from him. Like before, she mounted her horse, whirled it, and rode away, only this time there was just the soft fall of her horse's hoofs on the brittle grass, no wild little scream, no sound from her at all.

He made a cigarette and stopped in mid-motion, staring. For the first time in his life, his hands were shaking. He dashed the paper and tobacco aside, turned, and went deeper into the shade, found a huge old boulder, and sank down upon it. He was still sitting there much later when the musical chant of swinging rein chains brought his head up. Carus Smith pulled up, face drawn, a strange darkness in the moving background of his eyes.

"Howdy, Stormy."

"Howdy, Carus. You're a long way from home."

"Yeah. You seen Toni around?"

The tracks were there as plain as day. "Yes, she passed through here a while back. Get down."

Carus swung off, let the horse trail its reins, and moved in closer, hunkering down near Stormy and wiping a sleeve across his forehead with a long, despairing motion.

"Carus?"

"Yeah?" The boyish face came around, the eyes a little

bloodshot-looking.

"Why don't you marry her? You're in love with her, aren't you?"

Smith stared and his mouth flattened a little. "Why'd you say that?"

"Why? I watched you two at the dance. Was I wrong?"

Carus Smith made a throaty sound, half sob, half sigh. "No," he said, "you wasn't wrong. She won't marry me, Stormy. I've been . . . hell . . . she's been riding the hills and valleys like she's locoed for a week now. I been following her." Carus dropped his head, shook it dumbly. "She meets folks, and when I ask her about them . . . about where she's been . . . she hits me." He looked up. "Know what I think, Stormy? I think she's going crazy, maybe. She don't make sense. Not in what she says or does, she honestly don't."

Stormy felt for his tobacco sack, made a cigarette, watched his fingers, found them as steady as rock, and took heart from that. "Here, have a smoke."

"No, thanks."

He lit and exhaled, raised his eyes to the slot in the hill she'd come thundering down. "Carus, Jerry did me about the same," Stormy said slowly. "It's a little like catching a green colt for the first time. Takes considerable handling." His eyes were hanging on hillside heat waves in the middle distance, words coming up easily. They seemed to wash over Smith, who sat slumped and dejected, hat far back and the profile of his face set in dogged, bewildered lines.

". . . About like a colt until you get the halter on. Keep working down the rope, Carus. Talking smooth and easy." *Like I'm doing,* he thought. "But don't give up. Just like with a colt, Carus. Once you start, don't ever give up."

# CHAPTER SEVENTEEN

They were still sitting there when noon came. The sun began to slide off westward, and finally Carus reached for the tobacco sack. From then on Stormy's victory over the Big B foreman was assured. Only one other particular thing stuck in his mind.

"What's the colonel say?"

Carus handed back the makings and looked down, cupped a match inside his hands, as in winter, and held it for Stormy, who took a light, but didn't want to smoke.

"The colonel . . . he don't know, either. He's like me, Stormy. He's plumb twisted inside-out over her." A long ribbon of blue-gray smoke went past Carus's mouth. For a moment the younger man sat in stony silence, then he got up and dusted off his seat. "Y'think about them day and night, bend over backward to please them, say what you think they want you to say, and they either hit you or get on a horse and run off. I don't know what to think." He straightened around, gazing down at Stormy, whose face was coldly composed, thoughtful, looking past Smith at the hillside.

"I'll tell you something to try with her, Carus. It mightn't work, but it's worth trying."

"Shoot," Carus said heavily. "Anything's better'n nothing."

The blue eyes went to Smith's face. They were calculatingly hard. "Can you get her good and mad at you?"

Smith smiled mirthlessly, crookedly. "Can I? By God, that's all she ever *is* with me, any more."

157

"Good. Get her spitting mad at you, Carus, real roiled up, then grab her and just make love to her. Make her squeal."

Carus's eyes flew wide open. He looked too startled, too astonished to speak, then he cleared his throat. "She'd kill me. What kind of advice is that? She'd hate me to her dying day."

Stormy stood up, shaking his head. "I'll bet you a good horse she'll wind up marrying you. Want to bet?"

Carus was torn between hope and doubt. He didn't answer until he'd caught his horse and led it back to where Stormy was, then he screwed up his face in thoughtful resignation. "One thing," he said. "It'd make it or break it, wouldn't it?"

"It'd make it for you. I'll lay you odds on it."

Carus swung up and shortened his reins. "I don't like it, though. Feller shouldn't have to fight a woman like a cussed bobcat, should he?"

Stormy nodded his head knowingly. "If that's what it takes and you want the woman, why then you've got to do it."

Carus looked uncomfortable, uncertain. In a burst of resolution that was half despair, he threw up his head. "All right, Stormy. If you're right, you got a friend for life."

"And if I'm wrong?" The too gentle voice asked, the blue eyes like rain-washed agate.

Carus wilted at the thought. "If you're wrong, why I reckon we're both just wrong," he said. "Hell, I wouldn't hold a man responsible for trying his best and failing."

Stormy said good bye to Carus, caught his own horse, and rode southward without watching to see if Carus would quarter, pick up Toni's tracks, and follow them like he'd been doing, or not. He didn't care.

He made the ranch long after supper and Jerry got a meal for him because Cookie was down at the bunkhouse. She saw in his face that his spirit was light. It made her happy. After he'd eaten, she suggested another walk, but he demurred, suggesting instead that they sit on the gallery by the rosebush and talk, which pleased her just as much.

In a benevolent frame of mind, more from relief than because of overcoming an obstacle, he touched on MVP, its future under his hand. He outlined to her the ideas he had, and finally pointed to the clean yard where the silvery light lay, faint and soft.

She listened and, when he was finished, smiled at him with peacefulness glowing in her eyes. "I know you want things, Stormy. I know how you want them, I really do. Only Holystone would have been a better man to leave behind for the cleaning up." Instantly she saw her mistake. His jaw set, the dull ripple of muscle beneath the bronzed skin made a hollow under his cheek bones. He looked away from her, northward, through the fretwork of rosebush growth. She groped for a way back and found one in his talk of the early drive. Skillfully she brought the conversation around to that again, but something was gone that wouldn't return that night, and shortly afterward he got up and went inside to bed.

Sam Oberlin saw Stormy's black horse in the corral the next morning. He guessed that they would cut cattle from the herd that lingered just beyond the buildings, visible in the near distance, and sent the riders out separately to clean water holes, check drift on the plains above the valley, and made sure they would all be gone the better part of the day. Then he waited idly around the barn, near the shaggy old sycamore tree, until Stormy came out. When he saw him meandering down across the yard, he nodded in silence, dark eyes speculative.

"Today?"

Stormy went into the barn, turned just inside the door, and waited for Sam to follow him. "Yeah," he said. "Might as well be today."

"You wasn't gone long."

The blue eyes were reflective for a moment. "It didn't take long . . . what I had to do. Get your horse."

They rode through the cascading heat side-by-side, slouched and silent. When they flushed out the first critters, they pushed them upcountry, gathered in more, let the MVPs go around them, drifting back through the bawling movement with the smaller calves. It was an old story to them both, one they understood well. When one veered off, the other closed over. When the cutting began, there wasn't a word said but one set of rein hands moved to complement the other. Together they were a superb pair of working cowmen and they both knew it.

The hours limped by greased with horse and man sweat. There wasn't much dust, but there was cloying heat and cattle stench and noise. Calves bawled for their mothers, cows bawled for their calves. Men swore into the racket and horses blew their noses lustily, pushing, always crowding, working the animals to be driven north away from the ones to remain behind, forcing the cows and bulls back, slamming their legs hard, bunched up, to break the desperate charge of cows trying to return to their calves.

They got the cows clear of the thickets and trees, put them into a clumsy run, and kept them in it, their minds occupied with the need to run. Cow imbecility did the rest. The critters fled from the horsemen, forgot about turning back, ran until their tongues lolled, and their sluggish hearts beat with a thundering tattoo, low in their briskets.

By early sundown Stormy reined up. Sam came over beside him and spat, cleared his throat, and spat again. "All we got to do now," he said, "is post the hands around the young stuff until morning."

"Naw," Stormy contradicted him. "We'd lose some in the night. We'll corral them."

They rode back and corralled the animals to be trailed to

Fort Burnett, put up their horses, and had a cigarette together while the shadows deepened. When the other hands came in, they met them in the gloaming, saw their heads swivel toward the bulging corrals, and waited for them to speak through the deafening clamor of the cattle.

Holystone hobbled out front first. Garrulously he said: "Had t'put my horse in a stall, damned corrals all full. Means extry work dunging out." He peered down at Stormy and Sam. "You two make the cut all by yourselves?"

"Sure," Sam drawled. "A good hand could've done it alone."

Holystone chirped his derisive laugh. "Yeah," he said. "By God, I'd like to see one man cut that many calves away from their mammies and keep 'em apart. Boy, them little devils'd be back with their old ladies before the dust settled."

"Two men did it," Sam said.

Slim came up, paused, and looked at Stormy. "Is that the drive?" he asked quietly.

Stormy eyed him, said nothing, just nodded. Slim walked on past, cut in toward the bunkhouse, and Stormy watched him go.

Holk Peters dropped down with a self-conscious sigh, feeling around for his tobacco sack. "I cleaned out Cap-Rock Spring," he said. He held something out for them to see. "Look what I found over there."

Stormy took it, felt his heart lurch. It was a fancy little hair comb and he knew who it belonged to. He felt like swearing, but handed it back without comment. Sam's black eyes were fully on his face, which compounded his irritation.

"Sure pretty, isn't it?"

Holystone said: "Let me see. Well, I'll be dogged. Fell offen a woman. Probably Jerry's." He handed it back and squinted over at Stormy. "I had a funny experience today," he said musingly.

Stormy's gaze lingered on Toni's hair comb. "Well," he said with a ring to his voice, sharp and edgy, "if you're going to tell us, spit it out."

"Well," Holystone began, snuggling down lower in the gloom, moving his bony bottom on the hard ground. "I was over at the side hill spring where Sam sent me, y'see. Had the thing cleaned out and begun to climb up toward the rim above t'see if any of the others was coming by, and, by God, there sat a feller up there as big as life, like a damned statue. Like to startled the whey out of me. When he seen me crawling up there on all fours, he stuck a hand inside his long coat and glared at me like a cussed eagle. Sat there and glared. Y'can figure about how I felt . . . down on my all fours like that, scrabbling up the steepest part of that side hill . . . looking up and seeing two pits of brimstone in a leather face hawking down on me like that."

No one spoke. Holk Peters alone showed appreciation of Holystone's dilemma. His boyish face was turned back in a laughing way, but he was keeping silent, waiting for more.

"Go on," Stormy said.

"I just stayed down like I was and I reckon we must have looked at one another for a full minute, then he took his hand out from under his coat and put it on the saddle horn and said . . . 'Get up, *hombre,* what the hell you crawling around on all fours like a dog for, anyway?' I got up and told him I'd been cleaning out a spring just under the bluff and he . . . mind you without so much as another squeak . . . he turns his horse and goes riding off."

Sam said: "Which way?"

"Northward," Holystone answered. "Y'know what I think? I think he was a cussed preacher. Who else'd be wearing a long black coat in this kind of weather, but a preacher?"

Cookie broke it up by slamming the steel rod around inside the triangle over on the rear gallery. Holk Peters leaped up with the most alacrity he'd shown all day and Holystone kicked up dust arising.

"Wait up, Holk, dammit!"

Stormy and Sam walked together and let Holystone and Holk get far ahead of them. "What do you make of that?" Sam asked.

"I'll be damned if I know, Sam." They walked on. "Tell you what you'd better do," Stormy said. "Get up a little early tomorrow and ride the rim for tracks."

Sam was silent until just before they stepped up onto the back porch. "Probably another one hurrying south and stumbled onto Marais Valley."

"Maybe," Stormy said, holding the door for his foreman. "But I don't like to guess at things like that."

Sam passed on inside, doffed his hat when he saw Jerry at the head of the table, took his place, and waited for Stormy. The meal was a rather silent one, although Holk Peters and Holystone worked at getting a conversation going. It wasn't until they were outside, though, that either of them had any success, then Slim Thatcher, hearing them speculate on the comb Holk had found, approached them outside the bunkhouse and asked to see it.

Holk told about finding it and Slim studied it slowly, revolving it in his fingers. Without a word he handed it back and walked past the bunkhouse down toward the barn. Neither Holk nor Holystone saw how his fists were clenched. There was just one man left at MVP whose memory for hair combs included every one that Jerry owned. Slim also knew something else, that Toni Buttrick had tried his horse the day she'd been at MVP, and the animal had come back with several small cat-tail leaves in his cheek piece. The rest of it was too easy to figure out. He leaned on the corral with a hot tightness inside of him.

Back by the bunkhouse Holk Peters and Holystone turned toward the building. "Hey," Holystone said abruptly. "Darned if I'll play you two-handed."

Holk halted in the doorway, looking out into the night. "I

thought Slim was coming in." He turned toward Holystone, who was turning up the lamp inside. "Y'know something, Holystone. This place is getting so's it gives me the creeps. Something's going on around here. I don't understand it."

Holystone sat down at the table and fished in his pants pocket, brought out a greasy, unevenly shaped object sewed up tightly in very old buckskin. He held it in one palm and stroked it gently with the opposite hand, peering owlishly at Holk.

"You ain't even begun to see the smoke yet, boy. You ain't even begun to. Just wait a little." The puckered eyes swam in moisture. "And y'know what?" He dropped his voice. "There's going to be a killing."

At the sound of approaching footsteps, the ring of spurs, Holystone pocketed his talisman, and frowned at Holk. "Nary a word," he said.

Slim came in with a tired look to him, a downward drooping to the corners of his mouth. He cast his hat on his bunk and took his usual bench at the table. Without looking at either man, he spread his hands on the table top and said: "Deal 'em out, Holk."

The sounds of the game carried; it was a hot still night. Sam and Stormy talked a while around where the geranium bed was, then the foreman drifted across the yard toward the bunkhouse. Stormy continued around to the front of the house where he was arrested by a soft voice calling his name. "Stormy?"

"Yeah." He went over to her by the rosebush, saw her watching him, and suddenly felt the need for a drink. "Just a minute," he said, and swept quickly around the house to the office, groped for the door, and pushed inward. A stale, musty odor assailed him. He struck a match, walked stiltedly to the desk, found the bottle, pulled the cork, and drank deeply. When he put the cork back, he struck it savagely with his palm and let the match die, dropped it, and went back outside. His eyes stung. With a wry thought that it was no wonder Walter Proctor had died, he went back around the gallery where Jerry's white dress shone.

As though he had not abruptly left her, she said: "I suppose things will work out, won't they? Everything happens for the best, doesn't it?"

Some quirk made him think of Toni's face in the shade where they'd met. He was thankful for the darkness. It allowed him to recall Toni's twisted, frightened ugliness and, later, Carus Smith's misery and gullibility, the easy way he'd been twisted around Stormy's finger. His own knowledge of Toni's idiosyncrasy had enabled him to tell Carus how to get her.

"Yes," he said, "I reckon everything happens for the best. It's a little hard to see sometimes, though. Mostly it takes planning to make things work out best."

She jarred him with: "If it's a girl, what shall we name her?"

He sat in long silence and a strange thing happened. A wave of eeriness sought him out in the night, brushing with long, cold fingers across his awareness. He thought it must have been her question that had done it. But no—this was too unreal, too strange. He'd had premonitions before, but this was different, as though, through his unborn child, something final, something terrible and life destroying, was reaching for him, feeling through the blind night for him. He moved down the railing a little. The sad moonlight came through and touched his face, shone fully on his wife's face. He saw her strange expression and spoke in spite of himself.

"What's wrong?"

She said: "You look so . . . odd."

He swore, turned, and gazed up at the night with defiance and something almost like fear in his face. He swore again and faced her, shook himself inwardly, and felt the mood fall away. But it left its mark, whatever it was that the night portended.

Seeking something real to close his mind down around, he said, in answer to her question, that they should name the child after its mother, if it was a girl.

Jerry appeared to be having trouble maintaining her original mood. She drew a little shawl closer around her shoulders. "Yes," she said. "I'd like that." But her voice had a ring of hollowness in it. "Stormy, what happened just now?"

"Nothing," he snapped.

"But it was . . . something." Her large eyes went to the dim shadows of the gallery and back to his face. "Stormy . . . ?"

"What."

"Nothing." She got up and shivered. "I think I'll go to bed."

He stopped her. "Jerry?"

"Yes?"

"I'm going with the drive to Fort Burnett tomorrow."

"I know," she said simply. "Cookie told me."

He straightened off the railing. "Who do you want me to leave here with you?"

"It doesn't matter," she said. "Holystone or Cookie . . . it doesn't matter."

"Slim, maybe?"

"I don't care, Stormy." She said it with quiet indifference, crossed to him, and looked up into his face. "I don't care about very many things, really, but there's one thing I'd like to hear . . . sometime." They were close for only a moment. When he didn't speak, she turned away. "Good night."

"Good night."

# CHAPTER EIGHTEEN

Alone with his thoughts Stormy Merrill couldn't quite keep from bending long, searching stares into the shadows of the gallery. It had been a very strange thing, that premonition that ended up being something strong and menacing to him. He pulled back his lips and said very softly: "Come again sometime, you old tub of guts . . . I don't scare worth a damn!"

Beyond the gallery the moonlight was a soft-falling flood of silvery blood that eddied and pumped over everything. From the bunkhouse orange lamplight glowed and squat shadows fell. Farther away the bedding cattle were still making noise, many of them hoarse, managing little more than a husky bellow of animal grief at a parting that was more dumb-brute herd instinct than a need for a meal and a wicked-horned mother's protection.

On up the valley somewhere was Carus Smith and Toni. A glimpse of the girl's torn heart, bruised spirit, and nameless dread came to him and faded. Carus would take care of all that. By now he should be sleeping like a dead man, exhausted but triumphant. And Toni? She was hard and rational like her father. She would have realized by now that Stormy's way was the only way. By now she might be weeping, but she'd be free of the terror she'd known when last they met. She would know why things had worked out as they had—she and Carus. She wouldn't see yet that things were still possible between her and Stormy. She'd hate him this minute, probably. Well, let her.

Made as she was, fury was her secret undoing. He smiled. She'd strike him again, someday, and everything would be as it was before. Anyway, she would heal, and when she healed he would find her again and, finding her, knowing her as Mrs. Carus Smith from then on, with her child he'd have Marais Valley. Carus would kill her if he ever found out. She would give Stormy anything, Big B even, to protect herself and her child. Big B would fall into his lap like a ripe plum.

It might take several years, but he would wait. Wait in comfort, in fact. And later on he'd gradually replace Holk and Slim and Holystone, still later replace Carus and Deefy Hunt, Elmer Travis, Bob Thorne, replace Colonel Buttrick with himself and Carus with Sam Oberlin. Marais Valley. . . .

"Stormy . . . that you?"

It was Sam. Stormy stood up, shook the kink out of his saddle-numbed legs, and went to the edge of the gallery. "Yeah, what's kept you up so late?"

"I got an idea," Sam said. "I'll ride up on the rim tonight, right now, and be there come daylight. You can line out the drive and I'll catch up. All right?"

Stormy nodded, seeing the alert, anxious way Sam was standing. He was thoughtful for a moment, then he went still closer to the half-breed. "Sam, you're wanted for murder, aren't you?"

Oberlin's silence was long. "Better back up a little, Stormy," he said gently. "You're walking close to quicksand."

Stormy smiled. "The answer's in your face. All right, Sam, I don't blame you for worrying about that stranger. Ride up and make sure. I don't cotton to the idea of him, either."

Sam hesitated. "I wouldn't like to have a falling out with you, Stormy. Things are beginning to look good in the valley. It'd be too bad."

Stormy's thin smile stayed. "You won't have, Sam. Don't ever worry about that. Forget it." Then he stepped up until their faces were inches apart. "But before we're through in Marais Valley, there might be a chance for you to make a killing in more ways than one. I wanted you to know that. Wanted to be sure you knew how."

"I know how, all right," Sam said. "One way or another. Let's just let it stand like that for now."

"Yeah, see you somewhere along the trail tomorrow. And . . . Sam, if you find that feller and he's not just hurrying through the country. . . ."

"Don't worry," Sam said, striding away into the night.

# Chapter Nineteen

Stormy sent Holk Peters to ride the west wing just in case some of the more persistent mammy cows had walked all night to get back where they'd last seen their calves. He would much rather have sent Sam, but that wasn't possible. Anyway, it was gloomy enough out so that perhaps Holk wouldn't see any Big B cows if they were out there. Moreover, Holk was the least likely to suspect anything.

Stormy kept Slim riding the east wing of the drive and old Holystone pointing them. It was an awkward arrangement, but it couldn't be helped. He would have preferred having Sam at the point. The reason Sam wasn't present came to his mind. He wondered about the stranger in the frock coat. Outlaw on the run? Improbably a preacher like stupid old Holystone had thought. A sky pilot wouldn't pack a gun under his coat, wouldn't go for it when a surprised old devil like Holystone appeared. Lawman? He squirmed in his saddle, flipped his romal at the dull, shaggy backs just ahead of his black horse. Dammit, what was delaying Sam, anyway?

He looked westward to the black-shadowed, lonely faces of the valley's ramparts. Sam'd find anything, if there was anything worthwhile to find out there. Maybe, if it was a lawman, he'd be looking for Sam. Maybe just plain nosing around. Maybe he wasn't scenting up anyone in particular. Colville had been a long half year ago. Dammit, that was the trouble with the law. You could never altogether get away from its nosiness once you left your sign behind.

The cattle bawled because of the semi-darkness, but it was the best time to start a drive of young stock. They huddled up and traveled well, going by scent not sight, thus each one followed those ahead and the leaders followed the point rider and none made any breaks back like they would have done in broad daylight.

Holystone rode with one leg swinging, sitting twisted a little in the saddle so he could see the rolling sea of backs behind him. He stayed on the winding road, too, just far enough ahead so the critters would follow, not so far they couldn't see him or so close they could smell him. Holystone was an old hand.

Overhead a pale sky shown with soft clusters of winking lights. Some were blue, like water holes in early summer, some of faded amethyst. Others were cold and white, sharp-edged, brilliant. The sky was clear, the air full of night scent, grass and dust fragrance, the smells of a cattle drive. Stormy had the deep desire to push them, but only because he wanted them well beyond the busting back stage before daylight broke. He didn't give in to the urge, though, and after an hour all but a few refractory, dumb-stubborn critters ceased their bellowing. The herd moved easily through the stillness. He poked along in the drag, riding loosely and easily. He was still riding like that when the sky lightened, faded into a moist, ugly gray, then hurried through a whole spectrum of colors until it was the softest hue on earth and finally grew blue-pink, then just pink, then pink with a deeper red to it, and finally the red got a hot flush of orange and the sun came peeping up, casting a sharp light down across the valley. A new day was born.

Far ahead Stormy could see the herd stringing out, losing its bulkiness as the animals' vision improved with good light. He saw Holystone up there, riding at a slant, his stirrupless boot swinging to the gait of his horse. Off to the right Slim Thatcher was traveling parallel to the herd, but he rode straight up, tall in the saddle. He'd been thinking, Stormy imagined. Slim wasn't ever noisy or really talkative. Lately he'd gotten even quieter, like he had something big on his mind. Stormy considered this and cast it out contemptuously. A slipshod roundup boss would be a slipshod thinker.

He turned his head eastward but Holk wasn't in sight. There was a crooked creek course with willows along it in that direction. Holk would be beyond it somewhere. Anxiety quickened Stormy's thoughts of Holk, but no, even if a few Big B cows had tagged along, by now they were on Big B range and Holk wouldn't think anything of it.

He looked up where the sentinel buttes marched along in jagged relief beside the drive. Sam was up there somewhere. He hadn't expected to see him just yet, but he'd be glad when the half-breed caught up with them. It wasn't knowing that balled up a man's insides.

Holystone was rambling through one of those keening chants of his, and loudly. Those old-timers were half Texan, half Comanche. He gazed at the cattle. They seemed contented not to be hurried, browsing through the willows, splashing across the creeks, drinking when they wished and grazing all along the trail after Holystone pointed them away from the road and into the rising hills.

Heat worried itself inside his shirt, under his hat and pants, relaxed him, and until it did he wasn't aware that any great tension had been there. He made a cigarette, looked over it at the country they were passing through, and estimated how much ground they had covered, how much time it would take to make the drive at their plodding, leisurely gait. Three, maybe four days, there was no hurry. Smoke trickled up around the blue eyes that now looked in a lot of directions, yet always drifted back sharply to the overhead lifts where Sam was. It began to prey on him, Sam's absence, especially when they made the nooning and Sam still hadn't appeared. Holk Peters rode in and squatted with a bored wag of his head.

"There was a few old girls back yonder, but they didn't follow for long. Want me to stay on the wing, Stormy?"

His answer was sharp and made Slim lay a long, appraising look on him: "Sure, stay where you were. What'd you expect?"

They ate while the herd drifted northward, fanning out to fill up on Big B grass. When they were finished, each man went to his grazing horse, snugged up the cinch, and stepped aboard. Except for stops for meals there wasn't much to break the monotony. Stormy thought the drive was going too well. The first night out he'd told Holystone to make straws for the night hawking. Slim Thatcher drew the long straw. Second to go out would be Holystone, third was Holk Peters, and lastly Stormy drew the dawn go around. Slim ate in silence, and rode out. There wasn't anything to it when a herd was on good grass because, when they'd eaten and drunk, they'd lie down, rest their shanks.

Holk had his cards along. He took them out hopefully, looking from Holystone to Stormy. It was Stormy who finally grunted: "Deal 'em out."

They played four hands. Holystone lost as usual and for once Holk was held to a stand-off. He and Stormy played two more hands, then Holk gave up. He couldn't win and he didn't lose. They divided the pot and rolled in. Far out against the skyline Slim Thatcher sat his horse atop a jumbled knoll and smoked. An elusive something was teasing him and he couldn't button it down long enough to examine it so he shrugged and thought of other things—that comb Holk had found and Toni Buttrick's meander where cat-tails grew—Cap-Rock Spring, of course, the same direction he'd seen Merrill ride toward that same day. A lot of small things, divergent patterns made up something that was murky, unpleasant in his mind.

He was still up there, but hunkered down low upon the warm earth, watching idly for meteors when Holystone's horse came poking sleepily up the hill. It was time for Slim's relief. Holystone clambered down.

"Figured you'd be up here. How's things?"

"About like they'd be on a drive like this . . . quiet."

"Yeah, no sense to night hawking, really."

"Oh," Slim said, "you can't never tell."

Holystone agreed indifferently. "I reckon not." He looked out where cattle were dark blobs against the lighter ground, their scent and sound drifting up pleasantly. "If you was running this, I expect we'd have been to the glade by now or maybe topping out 'way behind Big B."

Slim was silent for a while with a dark and moody expression. "This is the right way, though," he said. "Give the devil his due. No hurry, no fuss, no shrink."

Holystone plucked up a stalk of grass and probed the gaps in his teeth with it, looking down the night. "I expect so, leastways this time of the year. Won't be any other herds at Burnett for months, anyway."

"No," Slim said. "And he's right there, too."

Holystone looked around. "Who, Stormy?"

"Yeah. He's not always wrong."

"But, pardner," Holystone said with sudden feeling, "when he *is* wrong, he's sure wronger'n all hell, ain't he?"

Slim looked at the older man. "What do you mean?"

"Well, for one thing, riding off like he did when Walt died."

*"Hmmm."*

"And on the roundup . . . him sending Sam to boss things. Why, hell, Slim . . . Sam'd take off before daylight and sometimes not come back till noon. Now then, y'know that's leaving too much work for me and Holk."

Slim's gaze clouded. "First time I heard that," he said.

Holystone shrugged. "Well, it's true. You wouldn't have done that."

"You mean Sam backslid on you and Holk, just rode off and lazed around somewhere?"

"I don't know *what* he did, but I damned well know he left me and Holk to do all the hard stuff between us. Cookie helped when he could, then he got so disgusted he just up and pulled out . . . went back to the ranch."

Slim pushed himself off the ground, cast a final look at the bedded herd, and turned toward his horse. He said: "I can't figure that out, Holystone. Sam's never backslid when I was with him." He mounted. "Maybe, because he's boss now. . . ."

Holystone removed his hat, threw it on the grass, and stretched out. "Boss or no boss," he said caustically, "no decent outfit'd keep a foreman long who left a short-handed roundup crew and went a-gallivanting around when there was work to do. And where in hell is he now?"

# CHAPTER TWENTY

Slim rode down to the camp, hobbled his horse, and rolled into his canvas. Up on the hill Holystone promptly fell asleep and was still sleeping when Holk came out hours later, shook him awake with unkind remarks about a night guard who slept, and took over the owl watch.

Stormy had the wee hours to himself and one thing above all else was in his mind: Sam. He was still worrying about the foreman when 4:00 a.m. came and he rode down to whistle the MVP crew to horse. The anxiety grew until dawn and it was light enough to see, then he saw the foreman coming wearily toward the herd from up ahead, northward. He rode out to meet him. Sam smiled wryly and swung his horse, waiting. Holystone, moving up to take the point, was waved back to the drag by Stormy. He and Sam fell in together at the point.

"What in hell took you so long?" Stormy demanded.

Succinctly Sam said: "Tracks." His dark eyes had circles under them. "Something's been going on."

A tightness encircled Stormy's chest. "What do you mean?"

"Well, I cut that feller's tracks all right, but I don't think he amounts to much. Looks like he sloped for Fort Burnett, went north, but hung to the high country." Sam shrugged, dismissing the stranger. "But I ran across a lot of other signs. Follered it all over hell's half acre. It always went back to Big B." He turned a quizzical stare upon Stormy. "One feller was follering another feller and the front one, he was poking around where MVP's range was being worked, just about every place he could go without being seen."

Stormy's constriction fell away and the light-headedness that followed almost made him laugh. Toni—Toni and Carus trailing her with his heart on the ground, as the Comanches say. He let a long wavering sigh erupt. "Sam, did you cut sign where those two'd come down a draw and crossed some range to a shady place under some oaks where there were big boulders."

Sam looked at him a second before replying, then his answer came slowly. "Yeah, there was a third set of tracks from down MVP way."

"That was me," Stormy said. "You've been following the Buttrick girl's and Carus Smith's tracks."

Sam grunted dourly hearing the relief in Stormy's voice. "Wild-goose chase?"

"Yeah, I should have told you. Well, no harm done. What'd you figure out about the stranger, aside from his route to Burnett?"

Sam's disappointment made him short. "There wasn't anything worth figuring out. He was riding a big roan horse, shod a long time ago. The way it looked to me he was sticking to the rims . . . maybe he wanted to see before he was seen. That spells outlaw to me. Anyway, when he left the rims where Holystone come onto him, he went like an arrow straight north. I'd guess him a stranger down here and when he bumps into Fort Burnett he'll slough off southward . . . shy away from the town like he shied away from the valley."

Stormy accepted it because it was plausible and because Sam wasn't the type to read sign wrong. He slumped in the saddle. They rode stirrup to stirrup for a long time in total silence, then Sam twisted for a long look at the herd behind them.

"Lose any?"

"Nope, not a head."

"Making slow time."

"I want to."

They rode in silence for a long time, both slouched and relaxed. It was hot. Sam kept nodding in his saddle. The heat curled leaves and made the creek water warm and oily tasting. When they were well beyond Big B, Stormy roused himself. He told Sam to keep the point, pick the easiest traveling route through the hills, and turned westward at the first lift of land. From back in the shadows of a scrub-oak grove he watched the herd meander by. Holystone came last, a big red handkerchief tied over his lower face, slouching along drowsily, great circles of sweat making crescents at his armpits.

When the last sound had died away, he swung a little southward and rode back a ways along the bluffs above Big B. Down below, the yard was still and shimmering, horses in the corrals stood heads down, and over by the house a slim, boyish figure in an eye-stinging white dress sat like stone in a thin spot of shade.

He made a cigarette and let the smoke burn past the dehydrated meat of his throat. There was an amused, rocky expression in the bold eyes. After a while he moved out into plain view with the dull, brassy sky behind him, silhouetted on the bluff. He waited, knowing her attention would be drawn to the only moving object in the stillness.

He didn't know when she saw him, but he knew she had when she arose and stood perfectly still, slim and straight, balancing almost, straining toward the middle distance where he was. Then she spun and ran into the house. Just for a moment a doubt lingered in his mind, then he forgot it. She couldn't ride far nor fast in that white dress. He reined back into the shade, dismounted, and sat with one leg dangling, waiting, smoking, and watching the blistered yard of Big B.

When a half hour slid by, he grew annoyed. He stood up and

smashed out the cigarette and frowned, cruelty running downward from his eyes across his face. Changing to riding clothes shouldn't take a whole half hour.

Later, when she didn't come at all, his anger was mixed with puzzlement and uneasiness. With a curse he mounted and headed northward, the anger coursing through him. He knew what it was and didn't like it. Woman hate. She hated him for what he'd done to her, for the alternative he'd suggested to shame and disgrace.

Contempt twisted his face. He'd make her get over that and it'd be easy. He'd make her beg him before he was through. Get down on her God-given knees—her Virginia-schooled knees—and beg him to be kind to her, not to tell.

The shadows he rode through to overtake the herd were long and soft and silently moving, contrasting companions for his savage mood. At that moment, with no bridle on his anger, he was easily capable of breaking Toni Buttrick with his hands, for there was, just this once, no clouding thoughts, no scheming business of mind to rein up his black and plunging passions.

Evening came with the shadow and the spent scent of the dying day. His horse's hoofs, moving through the limp grass, made no sound. Behind him lay the rusted green of Marais Valley, ahead was the sere upland country, parched, graying in the draws and arroyos, cooling with a tangy smell where the dead air hung. Only the deep-sucking trees up there were still bright and living. Texas, all shadowed and pure and liquid-running farther than any eye could see, was sighing after another summer day. In the twilight it was soft and clean until he looked off eastward, a little northeastward where dust billowed up, mushroomed out, where the MVP drive was.

He stared over there with a faint squint, for twilight was hurrying to meet the musky dust cloud. Sparks of crimson from the falling sun made regular wagon spokes through the spreading pall of dust. A faint, even breeze came gently to leaven the fury and sun-burned fever in his face, but nothing could gentle the fierceness of his gaze.

Slanting down off the ridge toward the herd he saw black mountains far off, away beyond where Fort Burnett lay: Comanche country. What he didn't know in his preoccupation, had no idea of, was that far behind him, blending into the deepening shadows, was a man, tall in the saddle, like an image of stone or wood, gazing after him, watching him through squinted eyes. A man who had swung away and tracked him to the heights above Big B and trailed him like a loafer wolf, slouched and cautious, since he'd left the herd—Slim Thatcher.

The herd was bedded and the cold meal partly over when Stormy came up, swung down, hobbled, and off-saddled. After dumping his gear in the dry, rustling grass, he went to the little circle and immediately saw Sam look up at him with a long, significant stare. He jerked his head heedless of what Holystone and Holk might think. Sam arose and followed him out where the cow smell was strong.

"What's wrong?"

Sam asked a question of his own. "Where's Slim?"

Stormy looked around, down where the two riders hunkered in silent hunger. "Slim? He's around somewhere, isn't he?"

"No. You'd no sooner drifted off back of those willows than I couldn't find him. I don't like that. Stormy, the closer I'm getting to Burnett, the stranger I'm beginning to feel." The dark eyes glowed. "What's going on I don't know about?"

Remembering Sam's comments about women, Stormy didn't answer, although right then was one of the few times in his life he would have like to have talked to someone, to let the words come out, hear them and see what kind of sense they made. He remembered the strange sensation back on the front gallery with Jerry and his mouth was dry.

"What's going on, dammit?" Sam repeated irritably, sharply.

Stormy looked up with a trace of the old anger in his face. "Holystone's medicine bundle's working, Sam." Then he laughed, making a sound like paper crinkling, and swung down toward where the game was, where Holk and Holystone were playing draw poker. There was Slim with four cards in one hand, the other hand out, palm upward, awaiting a fifth card. Stormy stopped still, looking at him. Behind him Sam came up and also stopped. Stormy moved in closer, but Sam hadn't recovered from seeing Slim stretched out there lazily, gawkishly, all long arms and legs, his hat on the ground beside him like he'd been there all the time.

Stormy went around where his saddle lay and jerked loose his ground sheet of canvas. He tried to catch Sam's eye over the heads of the card players, but the black stare was fixed on Slim.

Sam went closer, then halted again. He was wide-legged and glowering. "Slim, where'n hell did you go a few hours back?"

Slim's squint swung up mildly, his face was perfectly calm. "Got me and my horse a drink of water and attended to my private business. Is that all right?"

There was a quick tightening of the atmosphere. Holk Peters looked up, big-eyed, mouth agape. Holystone carefully put all his cards in his left hand, dropped the right one carelessly to his side, and craned his wrinkled face around and upward. Sam's scar reflected the blood-red, dying sunlight. A vein in his forehead was thumping solidly.

Stormy crossed to the little circle and dropped down with a grunt as though he was unaware of anything. He was close to Slim. Without looking at Sam at all he asked Holk to deal him in the game. It broke the tension. Sam stood a moment longer, then stumped furiously to his blankets and bedded down.

# Chapter Twenty-One

The next day Sam sulked and Stormy used up his meager store of patience talking him out of it. The cattle hit their grazing gait before sunup and held it until sundown. Holystone had the drag, Holk the west wing, Slim the east wing. Stormy rode with each of them from time to time. By evening, when they drove to a muddy creek, the tension hadn't dissolved but it had abated, at least outwardly.

The cattle wouldn't drink the muddy water. They bawled disapproval, went ambling in search of clean pools, found none, and had to be bunched several times before they would drink. After that they bedded down, disgruntled, glowering bovine reproach and in the last rays of daylight the MVP crew sat on horseback, watching them.

In the flowing hush of distance and shadows they could barely make out the twinkle of lights from Fort Burnett. The sight acted upon Holystone as it always did, rousing his spirits, roiling them with promise and tingling anticipation. He stared out where the pinpoints were with a loose, slack expression.

"Burnett again," he chirped, looking slyly at Stormy. "Second time already this year." He shut up as suddenly as he'd spoken, the memory of the other trip jumping out to haunt him.

Holk Peters repeated in a parroting way what he'd heard Holystone say. "They sure come through fine, didn't they?" He meant the cattle and no one answered him. Boy-like he retreated into abashed silence, his glance darting uncertainty.

Slim's gaze was unblinkingly on the cattle. It was a smoky, troubled look, one that had something intent but murky in its depths. Stormy, seeing how Thatcher regarded the critters, said: "We'll have been on the trail four days when we corral them tomorrow. See any hips showing . . . any shrink to speak of?"

Sam and Holk shook their heads. Slim raised his eyes to the sloping distance without speaking or moving, still wearing the peculiar expression.

Stormy saw the last of the cattle sink down and lifted his reins. "Live and learn," he said.

They made their last day's camp on a little breeze-caressed hilltop and Sam's long silence was broken finally when he and Stormy went to the muddy creek to wash. He kneeled, cast aside his hat, curled his shirt collar under, and reached up to his elbows into the water, cupping his hands. Without looking around, he said: "I'd like to know what that cussed Slim was up to when he rode away yesterday."

Stormy splashed in the water, blew out through it, and spat the residue of cattle-tasting droplets from his lips. "He told you. He had to go."

"Huh!" Sam grunted, puckering up against the anticipated coldness. "It don't take three hours to do *that*." He ducked his head and spluttered, came up squint-eyed, and said: "I don't trust him, never did. I don't trust any of them except Holk and he's too dumb to know up from down."

Stormy put his face low and let water run over it for a moment, then straightened up. "Holystone's got the Indian sign on you. The only one that had me worried was that stranger in the rimrocks."

Sam stood up, flinging off water. "I'll be glad when this's over. I got a feeling about things. How about paying them off in Burnett and hiring us a new set of hands?"

Stormy got up slowly, letting the breeze dry his face. It was almost cold where the water lay. He considered a moment before replying. "We might," he said, "but Holk's all right, and he knows the valley . . . the whole damned country hereabouts. Holystone, too."

Sam cursed violently. "That old . . . old *Pukutsi* . . . him and his *puha!* Someday I'll kill him. I don't like the way he sits around rocking with his damned eyes closed. Dirty old whelp!"

Stormy smiled inwardly but nothing showed on his face. Sam was looking at him. He shrugged, turning back toward camp, which lay below them a little. Beyond it, pale against the falling night, but with the last high sun rays reflecting off it, was a faint gray dust cloud. It held Stormy motionless. He lifted an arm.

"Look."

Sam turned, followed the upraised arm, and studied it. "Dust cloud," he said. "What's causing it? Wouldn't be freighters coming from the south or west, would it?"

Stormy shook his head in silence. Sam looked at him, caught something from him, and strained to see Stormy's face. "What is it?"

"It's coming from Marais Valley," Stormy said slowly.

"Cattle? Could Big B have a drive coming up? Maybe," Sam went on, "they got wind of what you planned and figured to cash in early, too."

"Don't be so damned dumb," Stormy said sharply. "It isn't big enough for a cattle drive's dust, Sam."

Sam strained his eyes southward. "Comanches?"

Stormy didn't deign to answer. The dust cloud was turning red under the dying daylight.

"Well, what is it, dammit?"

"I don't know," Stormy said. "It could be one of two things, maybe. A band of riders or a little dust devil . . . a little whirlwind. Sometimes, this time of year. . . ."

"Yeah?"

Stormy looked away from the mushrooming spiral, started to move down toward camp. "Take a horse and scout the hell out of the back country, Sam," he said, and left the foreman standing there.

The darkness kept increasing until just before they all laid out their ground cloths and rolled into them. When the moon came up, it was soft and white and as crooked as a melted ball of wax. Stormy lay under it wide-awake, waiting for Sam to return. Lying there and wondering about the dust cloud, he worried. He felt somehow that his destiny was approaching a climax of some kind. Great brushing black wings grazed his thoughts, made a chill pass over him like had happened that night on the gallery with Jerry. Only this time the contact was brief. It made him sit up in his sougan, staring over the camp and out into the night.

The stars sparkled, the masses of easterly and northerly mountains bulked, sharp and black, against the purple night and the splash of lonely moonlight seemed to float between heaven and earth, making a ground shroud of soft ghostliness. He groped for his tobacco sack and twisted up a smoke, hid the splutter of a match under his hat, and bent to inhale fire and life into the cigarette. When he raised up again, the blue of his eyes was almost as misty black as the night overhead and around.

A lake of something whitish, like a fallen cloud, lay down the hill where the cattle were bedded, and as he watched a heavy block of shadow moved through it. He stiffened. A man on a horse—coming from the northeast it couldn't be Sam. He felt for the ivory butt, unshipped the gun, and raised it over the edge of the canvas, watching. There was no other sign of movement and that was odd, for no rider, no matter how careful, could drift through a bedded herd of cattle and not rouse them in an instant. From a hilly shoulder of land westward, a coyote's sad and eerie song erupted.

Stormy swore. The words came sharp-edged and husky. His thumb clamped down over the knurled tip of the gun's hammer. The cigarette was dead and jutting from his lips. The diaphanous cloud down in the little meadow where the herd was bedded drifted, lifted a little uneasily, and moved on the breath of a sighing night breeze. The shadow wasn't there, and half an hour later Stormy lay the gun beside his leg under the canvas, ears as sharply attuned as a rat's ears, straining for the swish, the rein chain music of a horseman. His back ached from sitting like that.

Gradually from the west, and it sounded, a little northward, too, he heard a rider coming. That time he slid out of the canvas, tugged on his boots, and faded into the warm night, moving out where the horses were grazing and drowsing. He blended into the shadows and waited.

The rider swung down heavily and dropped his reins. He hobbled the animal that stood in docile patience, then tugged at the cinch without raising the stirrup leather, pulled the latigo with quick tugs, looped it through the rigging ring, unsnapped the poop strap buckle, and hauled off saddle and blanket, dropped them onto the ground before unbitting the beast. Then the man raised up, twisted, and saw Stormy standing there. They traded a stare in silence before Sam hunched over, spread his blanket sweat side up over the saddle, then crossed to the gloom where Stormy was.

"Well," the foreman said flatly, "*that* time it wasn't no fluke."

Stormy stood motionlessly, waiting, the iron band tightening around his chest again.

"There's six horsemen going toward Burnett and they're using our trail to get there." Sam turned, flung up an arm, and pointed southwestward. "About six, seven miles back, I'd judge, down in a draw."

"Any idea . . . ?"

"No," Sam said bluntly. "I don't know who they are and I didn't get down to scout them out. Too cussed dark and they were in a shale-rock draw where any noise'd carry a damned mile. It's too dark for stuff like that. If I kicked loose a little landslide, they'd know where I was from the sound. Even friends'd let you have it on a dark night doing something like that."

Stormy looked over where the dust cloud had been hours before. His brows were down in a concentrating way. "Big B?" he asked softly.

Sam squatted and made a cigarette, shielded the match flare, and looked perplexedly back the way he'd scouted. "Why? Unless they got business in Fort Burnett or . . . know we got some of their stock . . . why'd they be trailing us?"

"They might not be trailing us. Might just be going to Burnett. But there're only five Big B hands counting the colonel."

"How about the girl?"

"Well, yes," Stormy said, hunkering down, too. "You said you were careful when you picked up those slicks."

Sam swore. "Careful? I'm no kid at that game. When I catch a slick, no one sees me do it."

Stormy's irritability flared. "You tell me, then," he said.

Neither man spoke. Sam's cigarette glowed like an erratic firefly, bright then dull. After a while he said: "Why don't we push the herd down, starting right now. It's light enough with the moon. Get them corralled and sold and have the money in case there's something going on we don't know about."

Stormy's jaws bulged. He shook his head. "I told you a long time ago that's isn't what I've got in mind for us here. Besides, what could be going on?" Then, when Sam didn't reply, he stood up and said: "It won't be long before we start anyway. Be dawn directly." He turned, gazed down at Sam. "You weren't over by the herd an hour or so ago, were you?"

"Tonight? No, why?"

"I just wondered. There's no night hawk out. I'll saddle up and sort of sashay around them a time or two. You roll in if you want to. Get some shut-eye. I'll rouse all of you when it's time."

Sam sat there, cross-legged, watching Stormy saddle up, mount, and turn toward the bedding ground. His head swiveled slowly, dark eyes puzzled, apprehensive.

Stormy made one large circle. A few animals shook their horns at him, half-heartedly, sleepily. Now and then a critter would get up lumberingly, with creaking joints, and snuffle a grunt, stand silhouetted by the pale light, watching the solitary horseman making his big circle.

The ground fog had dissolved and the long-tumbling, downward slope of the country, outward to where it met the summer-dried valley where Fort Burnett lay, was softly clear and clean-looking. He completed his circle, saw a hillock, and rode up near its crest, dismounted, and trudged the last fifty feet afoot, stood there in his dark clothing, staring southward and mentally picking at the puzzle of the riders.

If it was Big B, it would have to be all of them, even Colonel Buttrick and Toni, and that wasn't likely unless—and that was where the worry started—unless Big B knew something. Could they be trailing MVP because someone had found a bagged-up, bawling, calfless cow? That was possible, of course, but he and Sam had driven the animals close to MVP to avoid that insofar as it was possible to avoid it. And Sam had said he'd taken only big, weaned calves. Their mothers wouldn't have much milk if they were five, six months old. They'd be just about dry. Sam would know that; he'd have thought of that like any experienced rustler would have.

If it wasn't for rustling then, what was Big B trailing them for? Toni? He considered it and scoffed at it. She wouldn't dare tell her father, or Carus, and she was too canny ever to think otherwise.

He frowned in deep thought. It probably wasn't Big B then. A posse? He cast that thought out as being ridiculous. Posses didn't originate in Marais Valley. They didn't come from the south, but from up around Fort Burnett where the law was. He'd bank on that.

That left travelers, hunters maybe, or perhaps a band of night riders. He went down off the hill toward his horse, mounted, and rode back to camp, hobbled the animal, off-saddled, and went back to his canvas. Sam was lying close. He raised his head up and looked across the short distance between them.

"See anything?"

Stormy frowned. The others were probably asleep, but it wasn't worth taking the chance. "No," he said. "Maybe they're horse hunters or a band of travelers."

"Or Big B," Sam said dourly. He lay back. "We'll damned well find out tomorrow."

Stormy didn't reply. He was restless in spite of the fact that he couldn't find any plausible reason to be especially uneasy over the mysterious riders. It was as though, somewhere around him, behind or perhaps ahead of him, a climax was awaiting his arrival. He could sense danger like he'd always been able to sense it.

He stared at the sky for a moment, then closed his eyes, and there was a brutal set to his mouth and jaw. He'd face a lot of danger for the biggest steal he'd ever conceived, a hell of a lot of it. And if it was Big B danger—Toni might wind up a widow and an orphan both before he quit fighting for something that had become more than just a dream to him.

# CHAPTER TWENTY-TWO

They whistled the herd up before daylight and began the long, leisurely downgrade with them. As though sensing an end to their journey, the animals strung out and Stormy, up ahead on the point, alone, saw one leggy, big-horned roan steer take the lead. He was high-headed and aggressive-looking. In any long drive a lead critter, self-appointed, that cast his shadow down the trail with an even gait, led his fellows.

Through the faintest of chills, the first any of the men had felt since months before in early spring, Stormy sought silhouettes of men on horses. Holystone, in the drag, was well out of sight, but westerly he could make out Holk Peters. Easterly there was an occasional glimpse of Slim. Of Sam there was no sign, but Stormy understood that.

There was a little rustle of movement in the air, a freshening sharpness. After the sun came up, everything was as clear as glass, sparklingly brilliant for once without heat haze. That would come later, after it warmed up.

The land dipped, leveled out, and when the dew evaporated and the first puffs of dust arrived, Stormy swung around, caught Slim's eye, and waved him up. Fort Burnett stood out like an old brown scab a few miles ahead of them. When Slim curved close, Stormy turned away from a long study of the town.

"You ride point, Slim. Take them out and around the town to where the corrals are. I'll go ahead and get the gates open."

Slim nodded, and Stormy booted out the black horse. The

town hurried up to meet him, prismatically clear, sharp-cornered, and looking as ugly, as bedraggled as ever.

A four-days' growth of beard wasn't much to hide behind, but he wasn't particularly chary any more. Not after months of being free and, he was sure, just about forgotten. A vestige of his old wolf wariness remained, enough so that his gaze was sharp as he rode. A big drive, especially in the off-season, would naturally arouse Fort Burnett. There would be lots of onlookers come out and stand around. No sense in being point rider for the whole town.

He skirted the town and swung down near the corrals, saw only the usual young boys and idlers who found excitement in every drive, and opened the corral gates. Remounting, he jogged up through town, mingling with the early morning traffic, riders and Democrat wagons in from the ranches, an occasional whirling-spoked buggy. At the Central Valley Saloon, he tied up and went in search of the buyer, Gregory. A barman directed him to a little house where the buyer lived. There a slim woman with deep-set, shy eyes and a brood of little Gregorys clustered around her like puppies who let him in. Gregory was finishing breakfast. He came into the parlor with a questioning look that vanished when he saw who his caller was. A hearty smile wreathed his face. He thrust out a hand.

"You don't waste any time, do you?"

They shook, and Stormy rolled his hat brim between his fingers. "The herd's coming in," he said.

Gregory's smile faded; he became all business. "Did you open the gates?"

"Yeah."

Gregory reached for his hat, pulled it on indifferently, and crossed the room toward the door making sucking sounds where the residue of his breakfast was. "Let's go down."

They used back roads, little more than gouged-out ruts, and

as they walked the buyer asked about the cattle. Stormy heard their bellows down by the corrals. It irked him because, in order to get there so soon, Slim must have brought them in fast.

"They look good to me."

Gregory grunted. "I hope they're good," he said.

# Chapter Twenty-Three

The dust was standing straight up where Slim, Holk, and Holystone were maneuvering the herd. A few head hung back, strange scents spooking them, but the big roan steer, head still high, full of confidence, swung in close to the nearest pole gate. Stormy and Al Gregory stopped, watching. The steer hiked unhesitatingly into the corral and the other animals, courage bolstered by his example, trickled in after him. Then the whole herd began pouring through the gates and the dust arose anew, strong-smelling and acrid. Gregory went over to the poles, leaned on them, looking through squinted eyes. Stormy slouched beside him.

"They're good, mister." Gregory turned with a pleased smile. "You see . . . it can be done. How long did it take you?"

"Two more days than MVP usually uses," Stormy said. He bobbed his head at the milling, bawling animals. "There's a lot of young ones in there, too. You notice that?"

"That's what I noticed first. Young ones'll usually shrink to beat hell right after they're taken off their mothers."

Stormy felt for his tobacco sack, made a cigarette, and lit it. He felt good; the little anxieties faded from his mind. Gazing out over the animals, he saw a lone rider coming through the dust toward him. Sam. He watched the foreman swing in toward the corral and a quick return of uneasiness riffled through him. Turning to Gregory, he said: "Look them over. I'll be back in a minute."

"Sure, take your time."

He walked out to meet Sam, who swung down and altered his course afoot so that he met Stormy, leading his horse and walking beside the broader man toward the hazed-over corrals. His face was darkly solemn. Whisker-stubble, black and dust-laced, made him look thirty years older.

"You find out who they are, Sam?"

"Yeah. It's Big B." The black eyes were as still as midnight. "Big B, all hands, even the girl. Did you do something to Big B I don't know about?"

"What do you mean?" His voice sounded hollow; the tightness was in his chest again.

Sam stopped walking, staring at him. "I don't know, that's why I'm asking. It ain't the cattle, Stormy, I'll tell you that."

"How do you know?"

"I already told you, back home. When I take a slick, the owner don't know it. All them calves was big ones. Old Buttrick and that baby-faced foreman of his could ride a week and never find a bawling cow. Nope, it ain't that. But what is it?"

The heat beat down through Stormy's hat. "Maybe just a trip to town," he said.

Sam grew exasperated. "No, by God," he said fiercely. "They're armed to the teeth and the colonel is leading them. They're out for war, I'm telling you. Now Stormy . . . you tell me why. I don't give a damn *who* I fight, but I want to know *why* I'm fighting."

Stormy's troubled gaze fell on a tall man in a frock coat who was lounging up beside Al Gregory over at the corrals. Something ticked at his mind but he spurned it. Toni? It had to be that, then, if Big B was trailing them for war. But Lord Almighty, she wouldn't do that. He thought of her arrogance, her green-eyed hardness, and knew with unshakable certainly the girl would die before she'd shame herself.

"Sam," he said finally and clearly, "I can't figure any reason for Big B to be on the prod unless it's the cattle."

Sam stood there, hip-shot, dark hands hooked in his shell belt, reins to his horse hanging from his fingers, black eyes fixed on Stormy's face without movement. "All right. Only thing we can do is wait it out. But there's five of them, Stormy, and only two of us." He made a wry face. "Thatcher'd count himself out, Holk and Holystone'd be as useless as teats on a bull. It's you and me if something happens."

Stormy listened, nodded, and shook his head gently, more puzzled than afraid of a fight with Big B. "I can't figure it out," he said.

Sam swore grimly and started toward the place where Holystone, Holk, and Slim were lounging in the dust with their head-down horses. "Don't try," he said, "but keep your eyes open and get the money for these damned critters as fast as you can."

Stormy went back where the buyer was waiting. His mind had been robbed of its measure of pleasure at having delivered the first fat cattle to come to Fort Burnett in a long time. Gregory was smiling.

"Want to go to the saloon and whittle the stick, Merrill?"

Stormy nodded. They walked away and the man in the frock coat, standing a little away down the corral, turned slowly and watched them depart.

The saloon was cool, almost chilly in a deeply shadowed and gloomy way, when they entered. There were only two old men in the room. They were seated at a worn table near the window where they could watch the ebb and flow of life beyond the glass. One sucked on a leaky pipe, unlit, that made bubbling sounds. The other one had an odor of moistness as though his prostate had turned to jelly. Neither spoke, just sat there and looked out of cloudy old eyes. The barman beamed his smile and waited.

"Beer," Gregory said, then lolled, looking up at the hard, stubbled face of Stormy and noticed its peculiar expression of tightness. "You can relax now," he said. "They're behind poles."

Stormy watched the mugs slide toward them. "I expect so," he said absently, probing his mind, knowing the things that could have brought Big B to Burnett on a war trail, but doubting firmly that either cause had brought them to fight. He had to force his mind back to the cattle. "Well, what do you think of them?" he asked.

"They are as good as any I've bought in a hell of a long time," Gregory said frankly. "How's two and a half cents sound to you? That's pretty good, considering the time of the. . . ."

"You can do a damned sight better and we both know it," Stormy said. He nodded at the buyer's untouched beer. "Drink it down. Maybe it'll melt the ice in your heart."

Gregory laughed and drank deeply, slammed the mug down, and said: "All right. Tops just plain tops without dickering. Four cents. That's absolutely tops, but I'm doing it for a reason. To encourage you to bring in more in the same shape so's we can both make a living."

"And you're making a cent a pound," Stormy said.

Gregory shook his head. "I wish it. I wish to hell I could tack on a whole cent when I sell them. I das'n't rig them for more than a half cent. Sending them to Abilene'll eat up a cent and shrink'll maybe take another penny. That's honest figures, Merrill." Gregory spread his hands out on the bar. "How do you want it, gold or bank draft?"

"Gold."

"Then let's go to the savings house."

# CHAPTER TWENTY-FOUR

When they hit the hard walk, Stormy saw two things at once. Toni Buttrick was standing with her back to him, talking earnestly to Carus Smith by a horse rack southward. He'd know that straight back, the high, squared shoulders, and the slim roundness anywhere. Why was she there? What was she saying? His hand brushed softly against the ivory-butted gun swaying at his hip.

The other thing he saw was Slim and Sam Oberlin, face to face and squared off. You could see men in that stance a half mile away and know there was something smoldering between them. Inside him something coiled up. He walked a little faster, and Gregory threw him an odd look, puffing along beside him.

Somehow, some way, things were coming apart. The solid structure of his schemes was being rat-nibbled and undermined. All right, get the damned cattle off his mind, the gold salted down in the bank, then face down whatever was building up behind his back. He longed to hear what Slim and Sam were saying, but he knew, as every gunfighter knew, that the longer men talked, argued, the less became the risk of bullets.

"In here."

He swung through the door into the quietude, the deep and abiding dignity of the bank, followed Gregory to a stretch of counter, and listened to words pass between the buyer and an elderly man with a wing collar and a pinkly glowing scalp, totally hairless. Irritability moved through him. He put his hand on the counter, crooked the fingers, and drummed softly. Gregory turned, studied his face, and guessed wrong.

"You look kind of dry. Why don't you just leave the money here until you're ready to light out?"

"I figure to," Stormy said. "Tell me something . . . is there anything going on hereabouts that would draw folks in from the ranches?"

Gregory blinked. "Not that I know of. No, why?"

"Oh . . . I saw a lot of ranchers in town, that's all."

"Probably provisioning. There's a feel of fall in the air, but as far as I know there's nothing going on."

Stormy directed his attention to the banker who returned from a cubicle, a walled off little room, with two flat canvas sacks and a heavy little box. The banker poured out the gold coins and began to count them aloud. Gregory's head bobbed in silent count and Stormy listened to the precise, incisive voice of the older man. Finished, the banker looked up at him.

"All right?"

Stormy nodded without speaking. The banker began to sack up the money. When he was finished, Gregory pushed a paper at Stormy for his signature. "Bill of sale," he explained. Stormy signed the paper and the banker looked down at the heavy little sacks. Stormy divined his thoughts.

"Give me a receipt for them and shove them into your safe until I come for them."

"Yes, of course."

He folded the receipt with sharp, decisive movements and looked from one of them to the other. "Anything else?" They both said, no. "Thanks, see you again." He left them there, gazing after him and crossed the room with the sound of his footfalls and his spurs solid on the oiled floor.

A soft haze hung over the town when he stopped just beyond the bank's entrance, looking up the roadway. There were more people out and stirring. Over by the livery barn a little group of idlers were standing with their backs to the sun, talking. Of Sam and Slim there was no sign.

He looked toward the hitch rail where he'd seen Toni and Carus Smith. They were gone, also. Southward a ways and across the road a faded, weather-checked sign said *Sheriff*. There were four horses tied at the rack, two bays, a roan, and a dusty, travel-weary, raw-boned sorrel. Next to the sheriff's office was another sign that spelled out *Nolan's Forge—Horseshoeing*. A man in a white shirt and a tilted, stiff-brimmed hat was leaning in the shade over there. He had a string tie hanging limply down his shirt front. It looked a little incongruous to see a man wearing a tie like that without a frock coat. A black-butted Colt lay close to his hip, thonged around his leg.

From the wide opening to Nolan's Forge came the sounds of a shoe being shaped on an anvil. Stormy moved off southward where he'd left his horse. Something was writhing in the back of his head, something he could sense, feel, but couldn't get hold of. He unlooped the reins and led the black horse afoot across the road toward the livery barn. The idlers before the barn let their talk dwindle away, watched him enter the cool interior without moving, and when he came out into the sunlight again, they were still silent and motionless. He cast them a casual glance, then started northward looking for his men. Specifically he wanted Sam, wanted to know what he and Slim had been arguing about, but the first MVP man he ran across was old Holystone. The old rider had a tangy, sour smell to him, his gait was unsteady, and his eyes were swimming blearily. Holystone peered up at him.

"Hah! Boss of the MVP hisself. Well, did you get a good price?" Holystone smiled in a vacant way and chirped his scratchy laugh. "Cowman never gets good price, but the buyers do. C'mon, belly up with me and we'll get a drink."

"Have you seen Sam?"

Holystone's smile faded a little. "Sam? Say, did you know Sam and Slim like to had a fight? Holk was down by the livery barn looking at used saddles and heard it."

"What about?"

"You." The old eyes grew cunning, like the eyes of a fox. "They like to got into it over you. Didn't know that, did you?"

"No, go on."

"Something else y'don't know, Stormy. Remember when I gave you that name, when you come riding into Marais Valley and brought a storm with you? Hah! Something else y'don't know."

"Holystone. . . ."

"Big B's in Burnett, too. The colonel and his whole crew."

"Why?"

"I don't know," Holystone said. "Holk was around a little bit ago and he told me they was here." Holystone looked up at Stormy again. "But anyway, Sam and Slim. . . ."

"What did Holk hear?" Stormy asked. "And where is Sam now?"

"He heard plenty. Is it worth a drink?"

Stormy's anger came boiling up, but he took Holystone into a saloon, bought him a drink, and waited until he'd downed it, gasped, coughed, shuddered, and made a cigarette.

"Holystone, damn you. . . ."

"I'm coming to it. They met . . . Sam and Slim . . . and Slim asked Sam where he went when he rode off and left Holk and me to do all the work on the roundup. Sam said it warn't none of his damned business and furthermore. . . ."

"All right," Stormy said quietly. "Where'd you last see Sam?"

"Sam? He was . . . let's see . . . where did I . . . ?"

Stormy wove his way through the men in the saloon without waiting for Holystone to finish. So it was the cattle, after all. It made him feel a lot better, knowing that. So Slim *had* figured something out, had he? That was fine because Slim had been itching for a bullet in the guts for a long time. The thing to do now was find Sam and get it all first-hand, find out how much Slim knew, how much Big B knew, then fight them, fight Big B six to two if need be. Slim? No cowboy living was a match for a gunman. Slim'd be easy.

He made a systematic search of the town, and once, down in a dark corner of the general store, he saw two Big B riders—Bob Thorne and Deefy Hunt, the latter trying on a fancy shirt with his back to the spot where Stormy stood, but of Sam there was no trace.

Coming out of a side alley, he stopped short when Colonel Buttrick stepped out of the sheriff's office, alone, grim-faced and craggy-looking. Stormy stepped back a little to watch and the colonel went over where the man in the white shirt was leaning against the outer wall of Nolan's Forge, stopped, and said something. The stranger's auburn head turned slightly, looked down at the colonel. His lips moved briefly, then he resumed his vigil, and Colonel Buttrick stalked down toward the livery barn.

Stormy felt hair at the base of his skull rising up. He swore under his breath and kept his gaze on the big man in front of the blacksmith shop. Why hadn't he noticed before? Gunman was written all over the stranger. Gunman, maybe lawman, the silly little shoestring tie that had seemed so ludicrous before assumed a new significance. Top-notch gunman and a dressy one. A lot of them were dressy. Had the colonel hired him? Stormy's heart was pounding in a solid, hard way. A quickening apprehension brought up his old alertness in a flash. Standing back in the alley's shadows he studied the town minutely, slowly, and the things he saw now and hadn't heeded before were glaringly, painfully significant.

What clinched his suspicions was the sight of Slim Thatcher escorting the cattle buyer, Al Gregory, out of the sheriff's office. Stormy's fury grew cold and vicious. So Slim *had* figured something; he'd probably recognized some of the slicks Sam had picked up, had worked with Colonel Buttrick, hand in glove, to get a warrant out for Stormy as a rustler. His anger burned in a tangent against Sam for being so greedy. Without the slicks. . . .

He saw Sam coming toward him up the hard walk and Sam's swarthy face was freshly shaved and clean-looking. It was Sam's eyes when their glances crossed that caught Stormy and held him. There was a cold and savage restlessness in them. Sam had been drinking, but apparently so far the effect had only been to heighten Sam's senses, not dull them. At sight of Stormy he swerved a little and stopped near the alley. Stormy wanted to curse.

"Where the hell have you been anyway?" Sam asked harshly.

"Looking for you. I heard you and Slim had an argument."

Sam turned his head, spat across the hard walk. A puff of dust arose where the expectoration landed. "Amounted to this," Sam said coldly. "Slim knows about the slicks." Sam's bitter gaze grew abruptly amused, but only briefly. "That was the only mistake we made."

"*We* made . . . ?"

Sam ignored it. "I figured him and old Holystone might remember some of those older Big B cows from handling them every year, but I never thought they'd recognize the calves. Well, Slim nailed me about it down by the livery barn."

"And?"

"I told him to go whistle up a stump. I'm foreman, not him." Sam's restless eyes burned with a queer intensity. "Did you get the money?"

"Yeah, listen to me . . . Buttrick and the feller who bought the cattle just came out of the sheriff's office, Slim Thatcher, too. There's going to be trouble. In front of the blacksmith shop next to the sheriff's place is a big feller in a white shirt . . . don't look over there now, dammit."

"What about him?"

"Lawman," Stormy said. "That or Buttrick's hired gunman."

The black eyes grew very still, hot, and dry-looking. "Go get the money," Sam said. "We'd better get to hell out of here, but I want to tell you something first, in case we get split up. I read that sign, Stormy, and I didn't tell you all I read. You and that green-eyed witch . . . I read all that where you two'd met. I told you once what'd happen. . . ."

"Save it," Stormy said. "We haven't got all day."

"You ruined. . . ."

"*Shut up!*"

Sam moved off the hard walk, away from the roadway.

"Big B's here about your blunder, Sam, not mine. Remember that."

"That don't change anything," Sam said curtly. "They're here."

"And we've got to pull out, fast. Now listen to me. That money's in the savings house up the road."

Sam turned sideways so he could see Stormy and both entrances to the dingy little alleyway. Now, with Stormy's words tumbling out, clarifying a plan, Sam suddenly said: "Hold it." His glance was fixed on something out on the sun-lighted road.

"What is it?"

"Trouble coming," Sam said, and his suppleness stirred, ran through the tough body and alerted every nerve and muscle. "Slim and Carus Smith crossing the road out there, and coming down from the south old Buttrick and three others I don't know."

Stormy moved, swung his body forward and sideways so he

could see what Sam had seen. They were closing in, even the big man with the severely straight stiff-brimmed hat and white shirt, ridiculous string tie moving when he moved. He and Sam and the others were the sole actors, but in a town like Fort Burnett, among people who had lived and rubbed elbows with death in many forms since infancy, there was no way to keep the feeling, the scent of impending violence and death a secret.

Through the emptying roadway he could see Colonel Buttrick and the big man with the white shirt and lashed-down gun—striding evenly, keeping pace with Slim and Carus, but from the opposite direction. Behind Buttrick was a short man with a nickel circlet with a small star inside it pinned to his shirt, beside him was a younger man, wide-eyed, dry-mouthed.

Stormy stiffened. "Sam," he said urgently, "the feller in the white shirt . . . I'll lay you odds he's the feller Holystone saw wearing the frock coat." The blue eyes grew intently dark and sharp. "Lawman, Sam."

Sam pressed flat against a building's wall. "Now we'll have to make a run for it without the money, dammit."

Stormy turned fully. Across the road two more men with nickel stars inside nickel circlets were standing together, slouched, hands on guns. There was no mistaking them or their reason for being there. They had the look, the stance. A short and squatty man was on the near side of the dusty roadway, half hidden by a wagon's tailgate, and even with him, but up on the hard walk, now completely deserted, stood another man, wide-legged, hat back, making no effort to conceal the sawed-off shotgun he was holding.,

Stormy's breath hissed out of him.

Sam said: "What is it? Behind us, too?"

"Yeah."

Sam swore. "Rangers . . . oh, hell." It was more disgust than fear. "I told you I had a feeling . . . back on the trail."

Stormy wasn't listening. The bank's door wasn't more than thirty feet southward along the hard walk, on their left. He licked his lips and they had an alkali taste. He looked down where Slim and Carus were.

Fort Burnett's roadway was empty. Wagons, buggies, even saddle horses were abandoned in the dust. A mantle of silence like a long, withheld breath hung over everything. Stormy was acutely conscious of the hush.

"Sam, I'm going to make a break for the bank's front door. I'm going to shoot Slim when I run toward it. You coming?"

In a tightly calm voice the half-breed said: "Go ahead."

Slim's boots made a soft sound on the hard walk planking when he stepped up onto it out of the roadway's dust. Carus Smith's footfalls thudded harshly. Stormy's legs bent and he sprang. Carus saw him, his mouth pulled up terribly. Slim stopped dead still. He hadn't moved when the bullet struck him inwardly, the cocked gun falling from his hand into the dust at the side of the hard walk.

Someone let out a yell at the sound of Stormy's shot. Sam Oberlin's wide mouth was skinned back. He snapped a shot at Carus who was moving sideways, digging for his gun. Sam's shot was wide.

Stormy heard the shotgun go off down the road from them and it spurred him on faster. A long splinter of wood flew out of the bank building inches ahead of him. A door loomed up. He tore it open and plunged into a twisted, narrowing hallway with a tiny square of light at the far end. Sam slammed into him, breathing heavily.

"This isn't the bank."

Stormy was moving through the dinginess when he answered. "Someone had my range. The next shot would have got me."

At the end of the hallway the door opened out onto a trash-littered alley. The stillness vibrated with sounds. Men were running, calling to one another.

Sam pushed him. "Don't stop!"

# CHAPTER TWENTY-FIVE

Stormy Merrill led the way across the alley, scrambled up a horse-high wooden fence, landed in soft earth where flowers grew, kicked his way past their detaining tendrils, and turned, mouth open, eyes bright and hot. Sam breathed a reek of whiskey breath into his face as he got up out of the flowerbed. "Horses," he croaked. "They'll cut us off afoot."

Stormy crossed the yard in a jog, flattened briefly at the edge of the house, then burst around it, and there, not fifty feet away tied to an iron post was a top buggy with a drowsing big brown mare between the shafts. Sam swore and pushed Stormy.

"No choice, c'mon!"

They raced to the rig with the sounds of pursuit closer. Stormy leaped into the rig and Sam tore loose the tie rope. The buggy was moving, the mare bolting with fright as Sam caught at the dashboard and hurled himself aboard. His weight made the buggy tilt crazily. Stormy had the whip loose of the socket and was cutting the mare's broad rear with it.

Chuckholes in the road made them careen drunkenly, then a gunshot shattered the stillness and a shout, high and wavering, erupted in their wake. Sam twisted, hung far out to look back. He yelled something at Stormy. Deeper gunshots sounded, carbines and rifles. Stormy hunched up his shoulders and headed for the dead-grass plain south of town.

Sam thumbed off a shot, paused, then fired twice more, and pulled back into the buggy with a scorching oath. He fumbled with his gun, punching out spent shells and cramming in fresh ones.

"Saddle horses, Stormy. We got to have saddle horses. They'll have a posse after us."

Stormy made no reply. He threw his weight against the right line until the mare turned a little, making a huge arc out on the plain beyond Fort Burnett. Saddle horses didn't grow on the prairie. If they were to get them, they'd have to go where they were and that meant Burnett proper, or just beyond it somewhere, where men were.

"Sam, I'm going to cut around to the west of town. First horses I see that're saddled I'll make for."

Sam swore some more, then said: "Go ahead. They'll get us in this damned buggy."

The mare held her gait without tiring. The wind tore at the isinglass curtains and Sam yelled suddenly: "They're coming! Hell, we'll never be able to go back around town. They're boiling out like flies!"

"Posse?"

"Yes! Feller with white shirt's out front. I can see a badge on him now." Blistering profanity, then: "Slow down! I want one good shot at that son . . . !"

"Watch for horses, you damned fool. We're coming around the west side of town."

Distantly guns popped. People were running across back lots to watch the wild race. Their distant cries and yells seemed to inspire the brown mare to greater efforts. She gave an almighty lunge that slammed both Stormy and Sam against the padded seat and went rocketing ahead on a second wind.

"We got a chance!" Sam yelled fiercely.

Stormy put both lines in one hand and eased back. Nothing happened. He knew the mare was running blind. "She's running away!"

By dint of strength alone he got the mare headed closer to the backs of houses, saw twisted faces and a few riflemen watching them, but ignored them when Sam leaned suddenly forward, brown fingers closing down vice-like on Stormy's lower arm.

"There . . . yonder! Saddled and ready."

But Stormy couldn't slow the mare. She was running in dumb-brute terror. No amount of sawing, of sidelining, or pulling, would slow her. A froth of bloody spume whipped backward from her torn mouth, splashed against Sam's cheek where Stormy saw it. He relaxed on the lines. If the mare's mouth was cut and she still wouldn't stop, nothing could stop her but total exhaustion.

"Jump, Sam! Jump!"

He didn't wait to see which way Sam rolled or even if he did roll. The ground came up, sun-baked, spiraling, and struck him a hard and staggering blow across the hips. He fought for balance, with his free hand pushed himself up, and raced with bursting lights inside his head for the two horses tied in the shade of a tree that were straining at their tie ropes, panicked by the noise of the runaway buggy.

As the rig went careening by, one of the horses broke his rope, lunged off balance just as a clawing hand snatched desperately at his reins, caught them, and a form catapulted itself astride him. He whirled with a whistling snort, legs moving frantically, and the searing pain of spurs in his flesh. He bolted.

A patchwork of dazzling light and smashing shadow inside Stormy's head died out, but his breath pumped painfully and his mouth hung open, sucking air. He twisted in the saddle, legs hanging free of too-short stirrups, looking back.

The posse was in full run, coming around the south end of town with dust jerking wildly to life under the horse's hoofs. Sam was half atop the other horse at the big old tree when the beast reared up with an ear-piercing scream and sprawled in a threshing heap. Sam was caught. The posse swarmed up and over him. Guns exploded. Long tongues of flame pointed downward at a man whose own gun, bucking in a dark and sweaty fist, fired back at them. And finally—stillness.

Stormy saw the man in the white shirt detach himself from the others. He and four other riders whirled away from the dust cloud that hung lazily above the sprawled half-breed and the horse he'd tried to ride, set their animals in a long lope, and took up the trail of the man who had escaped.

Stormy rode half turned in his saddle. He saw the five riders bunch up, call to one another, then fan out across the plain. Far behind them he saw something else, too. People swarming like flies under the big tree where Sam had been taken. He saw their swift and furious movement and knew what they were doing in such a passionate hurry even before he saw the dark form jerking upward until the head hung inches below a thick, stout limb.

The horse he rode wasn't a good one. He was stiff in the shoulders from too much jamming, corral-roping, or herd-cutting. He went up and down in a stiffly jolting way, trying hard, but he just wasn't capable of great speed. It angered Stormy. He looked at the sun, serene and barely moving in the cloudless sky, then ahead to the nearest break in the land. His heart sank.

It wouldn't take long. He had never known the feeling of defeat before. Now he did. It didn't frighten him so much as it disgusted him.

The Comanches had a way of doing at a time like this. It didn't always work, he thought ironically, his mind as clear as bell tone, but it was better than being run to earth like a worn-out wolf and nailed to the prairie with bullets. He tightened his hold on the reins, slowed the horse until the pursuit was close enough, then he leaned and bent the reins hard around. The old horse snorted, almost bending in the middle to obey. The right stirrup grazed the ground before the animal straightened up, lined out, and threw himself headlong at the oncoming posse men. Irrationally Stormy thought of Holystone and his knowledge of Comanche chants.

A man far down the prairie made a long, ringing yell, and two men, facing Stormy, raised their guns and fired. Only one of the bullets even came close.

He held his own fire until he was certain of the distance, and when he tilted, one of the posse men, facing him, veered off, racing northward. Another man who he dimly recognized from the way he sat a horse closed in. Stormy took instinctive aim and fired. The rider slewed half around in the saddle, went off sideways, and never once moved after he hit the ground. Cries of anger and warning blew out all around him. Several quick gunshots sounded. With them came realization that he'd shot Deefy Hunt of Big B.

The man in the white shirt slowed to a rocketing lope. He was very erect in the saddle. Sunlight dazzled off something worn high on his shirtfront. Stormy tilted the gun for a second shot, and, when he did, he saw a mushrooming paleness blossom from the Ranger's side. His horse gave a convulsive leap, a terrified squeal, and went low, running with everything that was in him. Stormy's bold gaze sharpened. He lowered his gun and squeezed off the shot. The Ranger's animal upended, dust flew, and far down the land a faint resounding scream went up from Fort Burnett.

He was almost past them, the old horse grunting with honest effort, straining himself. Ahead, the Ranger's white shirt was torn and hanging from him. He got up sluggishly and looked behind him where Stormy was, making no move toward the gun lying thirty feet away in the grass. His right arm dangled queerly at his side.

The rider farthest south was closing in rapidly. He had an amazingly fast horse. The beast's ewe neck was thrust far out, his long legs pumping furiously. The rider threw a long shot that went high overhead, another one that plowed up dust. Stormy turned, saw that this man was to be the one. . . .

He looped his reins, no longer caring, a welter of wildness searing through him. When the man was within range, he lifted the ivory-butted pistol very deliberately and at that precise moment, when his thumb rested with its sweat grease on the hammer, the hurtling horseman fired.

That time Stormy knew, for the old horse changed leads in a convulsive way and slowed, stumbled, then collapsed. He jumped clear, stopped his stabbing run, and turned to face the posse man. He recognized the horse first—the one he'd ridden into Marais Valley, fastest horse in West Texas—then the rider, the lean, intent, hatchet-faced rider: Colonel Buttrick.

Another shot. Dirt plumed upward making him wince. His own aim was spoiled, the bullet went high. He snagged the dog and tugged it back, but the colonel was close. The colonel fired first, his third shot. It was like being kicked in the belly by a fourteen-hundred-pound mule. The wind burst out of him. He caved in, folded over in spite of himself, and saw something whitish, wet, and shiny. "Damned . . . rib bone."

# CHAPTER TWENTY-SIX

When Stormy opened his eyes, it was dark with people—hushed, hot-eyed, staring people. There was a thick woodenness to his tongue and the sun overhead dug with blunt fingers for the cords behind his eyes. Holystone, Holk Peters, all white and sick-looking. Greenish-lipped Elmer Travis.

The colonel, too, standing there with his thin bloodless mouth, his eyes burning with hot light, unpleasant to look into. Slim Thatcher standing there. Slim. . . . He strained to see better. It couldn't be . . . but it was. Slim. He thought he'd killed the squint-eyed beanpole. Slim was leaning on a big stick, white in the face, mouth flat and sucked back to control pain. Well, he'd hit him then, anyway. He'd wanted to kill him—but to hell with it now. Slim made him think of Jerry. He closed his eyes and saw them riding together over Marais Valley in the twilight, maybe talking, maybe remembering. MVP, Jerry, Slim, a kid they'd raise.

He opened his eyes and a shock went through him, sharpening the dimming vision. Toni. What a hell of a place for a woman to be—no, she'd want it that way. His eyes held hers. She was as pale as that Ranger's shirt had been, white and sort of rust-gray around the mouth, circles under the green eyes making them greener, larger. *All right, Toni, stand there and stare. It's all right. . . .* Something inside him wouldn't work, and he couldn't say it to her, but he thought it to her. *Stand there and watch a man die, Toni, that ought to make you feel revenged. Watch his hopes die first, then his spirit, then his body. See his pride die. No, that's already dead. Well, see all the rest of it desert him, leak away, wind up in a stinking hole like Fort Burnett.*

A sheen of oiliness appeared over her green eyes. The long mouth moved, then grew hard and steady.

Carus Smith was looking at him and of them all he alone kneeled and touched Stormy's chest, lightly with one hand.

"Stormy. . . ."

It made beads of sweat pop out on Stormy's face, but he strained until the dimness receded a little and a faint croak came out. "Carus . . . ?"

"Rangers, Stormy. Ranger captain recognized you from Colville. Said you killed a man over there. They watched you day and night until reinforcements came. They saw what Sam was doing with Big B calves. I don't know what to say, Stormy. I always judge a man by the way he treats me. And you did me a favor, you know. That day . . . you'll know what I mean. Me and Toni. We're married, Stormy. . . ."

Stormy let his head fall back. The green eyes were glassy above him until a shadow wafted softly over his face, and he strained hard to see it. Sam dangled up there. So they'd brought him back to the tree. Figured they'd give him a send off like Sam got. They'd lose there. He wouldn't last that long.

"Stormy, you hear me?"

Slim's voice. He couldn't hear the words too well. It sounded like Slim was talking under water.

"Drive the cattle slow," Slim was saying in that bubbling way. "Keep things up . . . early drives and fat critters. You were a good teacher, Stormy. I'll remember you. I'll take care of Jerry. . . ."

*Remember me, you strung out son-of-a-bitch! I tried to kill you!*

"That was a close shot, Stormy, through the hip, but missed the bone. No hard feelings, though. S'long, Stormy. S'long."

The gently swaying shadow came gyrating ever so gently around and around and grew deeper, fuller, darker. . . .

# ABOUT THE AUTHOR

**Lauran Paine** who, under his own name and various pseudonyms has written over a thousand books, was born in Duluth, Minnesota. His family moved to California when he was at a young age and his apprenticeship as a Western writer came about through the years he spent in the livestock trade, rodeos, and even motion pictures where he served as an extra because of his expert horsemanship in several films starring movie cowboy Johnny Mack Brown. In the late 1930s, Paine trapped wild horses in northern Arizona and even, for a time, worked as a professional farrier. Paine came to know the Old West through the eyes of many who had been born in the previous century, and he learned that Western life had been very different from the way it was portrayed on the screen. "I knew men who had killed other men," he later recalled. "But they were the exceptions. Prior to and during the Depression, people were just too busy eking out an existence to indulge in Saturday-night brawls." He served in the U.S. Navy in the Second World War and began writing for Western pulp magazines following his discharge. It is interesting to note that all of his earliest novels (written under his own name and the pseudonym Mark Carrel) were published in the British market and he soon had as strong a following in that country as in the United States. Paine's Western fiction is characterized by strong plots, authenticity, an apparently effortless ability to construct situation and character, and a preference for building his stories upon a solid founda-

217.

tion of historical fact. *Adobe Empire* (1956), one of his best early novels, is a fictionalized account of the last twenty years in the life of trader William Bent and, in an off-trail way, has a melancholy, bittersweet texture that is not easily forgotten. In later novels like *Cache Cañon* (Five Star Westerns, 1998) and *Halfmoon Ranch* (Five Star Westerns, 2007), he showed that the special magic and power of his stories and characters had only matured along with his basic themes of changing times, changing attitudes, learning from experience, respecting Nature, and the yearning for a simpler, more moderate way of life. His next **Five Star Western** will be *The Story of Buckhorn.*